Don't Let Life Bring You Down

by Joe Lynam

Published in 2012 by FeedARead Publishing

British Library C.I.P.

A CIP catalogue record for this title is available from the British Library.

Chapter One

Most ceilings look the same. White, or maybe cream, with few visible strokes or marks left behind by the paintbrush. Except for those old-fashioned ones where the painter would leave loads of blobs of paint all over the ceiling. If you looked carefully at those kinds of ceilings you could see faces and figures, like when you look at clouds. My grandparents used to have one of those ceilings in the room which I used to stay in when I visited them as a boy. During quiet moments I made visual stories of the people and animals I could see above me.

Nowadays I still often lay in my bed and stare at the white ceiling above me. Sometimes for a few minutes before going to sleep. Sometimes for a bit longer before I get up. Usually it's to ponder the day that just was or the one that's going to be. Or I might think about the good times and the bad. And the fun moments and the sad.
Today's a little indifferent, but I've felt like that a lot recently for different reasons. I don't really know how I'm feeling. I've laid here for maybe an hour now thinking about nothing, just staring into the whiteness, avoiding the day that awaits me.

Things used to seem so clear before, not only when I was a child being spoilt by my grandparents, but even just a few weeks ago. Somewhere the path got misty and now I don't know what to do or how to feel. It makes me wonder if there's someone, a higher power, pulling the strings of our lives. And are they doing it to help us or guide us? Or just to confuse and torment us?

How did things get like this? All I wanted to do was help but things have gone a little differently and now I've let things go too far. I did something bad last night, I'll tell you about it in time, but first I'll start from the beginning.

My name's Doug by the way.

Chapter Two

It's a bright sunny morning. Looking up between the few clouds I see a blue autumn sky. It's one of those autumn days that make you think it's the last one of its kind until the spring. From now on things will get colder and darker. But for now the trees are shining in the sunlight, the leaves enjoying their places upon them before it's their time to fall. Looking around me at the bus stop it seems that everyone has been cheered by this beautiful start to the day. I know I have.

I'm going to take the bus to work today. Though I am beginning to wish I wasn't. I'm going to be late again, I can feel it. I look again at my watch, it's five past. Where is the damn bus? I think to myself. People pay so much money for public transport and for what? It's rarely on time, it's rarely clean and there's rarely enough space for everyone to get on board, never mind be comfortable. It makes me wonder where the money goes. But people need public transport, so they'll always pay for it. But maybe people should stop paying the top price until they receive top service. If questions are asked by ticket inspectors then people can ask their own questions. For example, when will there be value for money? It always baffles me that fares are higher during peak-times when the transport is busier and therefore the service is of lower quality. Why isn't the fare lower during those times when people are herded in like cattle into a late arriving bus or train? Why pay more for a worse service?

I can't be late again. I was late just a few days ago; it's becoming a regular thing. Soon they'll start planning the work duties around me arriving late. And no one's going to believe the bus was late, will they? Even though it is.

Usually I have a genuine reason for being late for work. The bus was late, or even cancelled, the traffic was terrible, there was an accident. Those have all happened to me before, I can't use them again, can I? I have to think of a good excuse and ways of defending it in case the boss gets angry with me.

I've always wanted to use the one about the bus breaking down. With the driver trying to restart the engine, deciding we have to get off and then waiting for another bus, I think that could allow me to be about 30 minutes late. And I can blame it all on Transport for London.

Or I could say the bus was involved in an accident. The paramedics wanted to take everybody to the hospital for checks but I told them I was ok, despite the pain in my shoulder. If I then turned up for work holding my shoulder and with a pained expression on my face I could even get some sympathy too.
I'll say the bus driver apologised to everyone for arriving late and let us have a free journey in order to placate the angry passengers. Yeah, I think angry passengers could be a good idea. If I say everyone was shouting and threatening to riot then that would deflect some of the focus away from me. Upon arriving at work I could say, "I know I'm late, but I'm probably lucky to be here at all!" I could even tell them to look

up the story on the news and then look surprised when they don't find anything.

The bus being late is actually the truth and if I tell the truth I won't be wrong, will I? But who ever believes the truth? I'll have to defend this one to the hilt. I'll say that no one ever mentions anything when I'm early, only when I'm late. If I'm not praised for the positives then don't criticise the negatives.
These aren't even excuses, this is the truth. There's no way anyone could deny this. I just hope I remember it all in the heat of a possible argument.

Here comes the bus. A few schoolgirls are stood in front of me, I'll let them get on first, my gentlemanly act done for the day. I look down at them, they're all chewing gum and blowing bubbles with it. They're speaking a language which might as well be foreign to me for what I can understand of it. I only manage to make out 'hot', 'fit', 'ride' and some boys' names. I probably don't want to know what they're talking about. What's more important at the moment is that they don't actually seem to be getting on to the bus. They're standing at the stop, next to the open door but not getting on. My eyes quickly move from the girls to the closing door of the bus. I, quite athletically, it must be said, launch myself past the girls towards the bus door, which smacks me in the face. The driver is now looking at the passing traffic out of his window on the other side. He can't see me. He'll hear me though. I bang on the door of the bus. Nothing. Then I bang and shout, 'Oi!!' Still nothing. Until the driver turns from that window to the one straight ahead and starts to drive the bus forwards. 'He's going without me.' I think. I was standing right here and he didn't see me. He didn't even hear me banging. Or he chose not to listen.

How could he do this? I give the bus a cold stare as it leaves me, hoping the driver's looking at me in his mirror. I look at the bus' number plate and make a note of it in my mind. Maybe I could report the driver. I might even get some kind of compensation that way. That would be a lengthy process though and would involve too much bureaucracy. I'd prefer something more immediate. Maybe I'll head to the bus depot after work, find out which driver drives this bus and confront him. Or maybe I'll just let down his tyres.

Almost as soon as the bus leaves the bus stop it leads to a red traffic light about 50 metres ahead. I start to wonder if I could run and manage to make it to the next bus stop ahead of the bus. It's currently stuck at the back of the queue and I'm not convinced it will even make it through these lights without them turning to red again. The bus stop's not that far away. If I run quickly I think I'll do it. And that will show that damn driver. Oooh, yeah, I can imagine his face now as he sees me step on to his bus. Yep, that's it, that's tipped the scales, that's the deciding factor. I had a small doubt as to whether I'd do it but the thoughts of the driver's bemused face and my face of justice, pride and, not least of all, victory have convinced the petty mind inside of me. Let's do it.

But let's do it quickly. I can't hang around or I'll definitely arrive after the bus. I just need to decide on one more small thing. Shall I just run away immediately or shall I do it a little more gradually? What will the people around me think if I suddenly just sprint away from the bus stop? Maybe they'll think I've just robbed someone and I'll be chased. I suppose that would make me run quicker and beat the bus.

I decide to walk away from the bus stop and after a few metres I run. I don't begin with a jog, I sprint right away. And I feel good. I've got a good speed and I can already see the finishing line up ahead. The only problem is the traffic in the road to my right has started moving. Very soon I'll see the bus approach me. Or not, if the traffic light changed back to red before the bus passed it. I can't look round, that will slow me down too much. Wait, there's the bus now. It's passing me, though not flying past me thankfully. I look ahead to the bus stop and see many people there waiting. I hope they're waiting for the same bus as me. That way it'll take a while for everyone to get on and the bus will be at the stop longer, giving me time to catch it up.

And that's what happens. Around eight people get on the bus and the last of them is me. I swipe my oyster card and look at the driver. I tell him, "It was nice of you to stop this time. I made it after all"

Through the glass dividing us I can only hear a muffled "What?"

"Didn't you see me run here from the last stop?"

I begin to walk away from the door towards the seats, content with the point I feel I've made.

"Go sit down, you prick, you're wasting everyone's time." he tells me before preparing to restart the bus' journey.

"You're the prick, mate." I say with the intention of being quiet enough so that the driver won't hear but loud enough for the other passengers to hear and know that I've given something back.

But it seems I've said it loud enough. Behind me I hear the small door to the driver's compartment open. I turn around and see his head leaning out along with one of his legs coming out of the doorway and down on to the floor. I suddenly feel my breakfast rising up to my throat and my knees turning to jelly.

"What did you say? he says. "If you give me any more of that I'll throw you off this bus, alright?"

He stares at me and maintains it for a few seconds. I stare back but without the same intensity I imagine.

I start to believe that he didn't intentionally drive off from the last bus stop. He probably didn't see me trying to get on. Should I explain the whole thing to him? Maybe that would placate the aggressive situation we have now.

I decide that for now the best thing to do would be to turn around. I look at the faces of some of the other passengers and they look right back at me. I quickly look away. I find a seat next to the window. I sit down, look ahead and see the driver's eyes in the mirror looking at me. I've got a 30 minute journey ahead of me here. Maybe I should get off at the next stop and wait for the next bus. No, I'll go sit upstairs instead.

Chapter Three

Sitting alone upstairs on the bus, hoping no one will sit next to me, I just need a little peace for myself. Sometimes I hate having to share my space. I never get to sit alone on the bus; someone always comes along and plants their big arse next to mine. Usually it's some kind of weirdo. Please I think I deserve it today, just this once. The seats around me are starting to fill up, soon there won't be any spare ones left, and I'll have to share.

Why didn't I stand up for myself? I can't answer that, I don't know how to. I tried to be a smart-arse and bottled it when I got confronted. Made snide remarks to the driver and froze when he gave some back. I shouldn't have said to him what I did. Or at least not in the way that I did. That was my mistake. That put me in the wrong when in the first place it was the driver who was wrong. Now I'm sitting here cringing at what happened. Embarrassed at leaving my backbone behind when I got on the bus.

But then why should I? It was he who was at fault and it was he who was being aggressive. And he's a bus driver being aggressive to a passenger, that's not right. There are codes of conduct against that kind of thing. Shall I demand to know his name and employee number or something? That could put me in a big light, show that I'm a big man who's going to do something about this. And without violence or any physicality too. I could even say I'm a lawyer and that he's going to get a shitstorm for what he's done. Or I could say I work for Transport for London and I can get him sacked just like that (I would click my fingers). I'll go back down there when I get off.

Here comes a man up the stairs, please don't sit here. He looks like he just stepped out of a drug den and didn't wash himself. He's got unbrushed grey hair tied into a pony tail and is dressed from head to toe in denim. Oh, not toe, he's got a pair of brown suede shoes on. His eyes are twitching from one side of the aisle to the other. One side of his mouth is half open, like he's smiling on one side. He must be on something this fella. I almost hope he is. Otherwise what kind of nutter is he?

Phew, he sat somewhere else.

I caught a glimpse of him sitting down. He was nodding very enthusiastically to the woman he was joining. Now he's turning around, he's going to see me looking at him. I don't look away, I can't seem to. I want to see what he's turning around for. Is he going to choose someone at random and start shouting at them? Seems like the sort of thing he'd do. He doesn't seem to be looking around for anything, just staring into the space. I don't think he even realises there are 10 or so people behind him. Or he doesn't understand what we're all doing here.

I can see another man now standing at the top of the stairs. He looks down to the few spare seats at the front and then to the back. He then bends his neck forward as if to get a different view of the back section of the bus. Does he think we're hiding spare seats from him back here? Why does he keep looking? Just sit somewhere. Not next to me though.

He looks down again at the front of the bus. A couple are sitting together arm in arm on one seat and on another is the first man, who's now sitting alone, the woman he was sitting next to leaving him to sit somewhere else. The man's face suddenly has an expression of panic. He turns around to the steps below him and sees several people walking up and urging him to make way for them. He seems to gulp and intake a large breath as if he's about to do a bungee jump. He steps into the aisle and walks towards the back section of the bus.

The man looks very nervous, like he's afraid to make eye contact with anyone or accidentally touch anyone. What does he have to be nervous about I wonder? Is he fleeing the scene of a crime? Is he about to commit a crime? Maybe he's one of those compulsive people who have to have everything a certain way. Maybe he can only sit on a bus with 14 passengers. More than that and he'll start freaking out. He's already passed a number of available seats but has decided to keep walking. He hasn't decided to sit next to me, has he? I think I could put him off from sitting next to me if I look aggressive and hostile enough. He reaches my row and I give him a look that tells him he'll get so much trouble if he sits next to me. He sits himself down in the seats opposite. He gives a tiny glance over to me to check I'm still giving him the look. I'm not though, I don't need to anymore, job's done.

Nearly all the seats are full now; I might make it to the end of my journey in peace.

But we're at another bus stop now and I can see people getting on from the window. A woman comes up the steps and looks around for an empty seat. She's looking over towards me, this could be interesting. She's pretty, I'd allow her to sit here, that would be no problem. The difference between sharing your seat with a pretty woman and anyone else is huge. I'm not going to do anything; I have a girlfriend I'm very happy with. This is just companionship, someone to share my seat with. Before I can give her a smile she sits down a few rows in front of me. That was disappointing. Never mind, more fish in the sea and all that.

And here comes another. She's medium height, blond hair, quite pale skin, looks foreign. Wearing a skirt and tights. Not a bad body. Not as good looking as the other but I'm not fussy. I keep check on her with the corner of my eye; I don't want to seem too obvious. But when the time's right I'll give her a proper look to let her know I'm interested then I'll give her a few more glances once the bus starts moving again and hope she does the same. Oh, but she's sitting behind me. I can't be dealing with that. If she was sitting in front or alongside me then I could do something and still maintain some control, especially if things went wrong and I needed to play it cool. If she caught me looking at her and was put off then I could pretend I was looking at something outside the window. But now she's behind me I'll have to turn around all the time. And what would my excuse be? 'I want to see the traffic behind us.' Or 'I want to make sure the bus isn't being followed.' No, I'll forget about her.

This is strange. I never get to sit alone on the bus for this long. Why is no one sitting next to me? Do I still have that hostile expression on I had earlier? Maybe people are looking at me and thinking, 'I'm not sitting next to him, might catch something.' I don't understand it. I thought I looked reasonably presentable in the mirror when about to leave the flat. I hadn't showered admittedly but I didn't think that was immediately noticeable.

And then suddenly someone is sitting their self next to me. Half next to me maybe. He's sitting almost with his back to me and his legs in the aisle, as if wanting to show people that he isn't with me. Or to show that he's not going to do like everyone else on the bus, i.e., sit straight, face the front and without talking to yourself. He's not doing any of that. He's continuously mumbling to himself about something I can't catch. I'm trying my best to ignore him. I'm staring out of the window at the mundane urban view, I'm making a shopping list in my head, I'm pretending to be asleep.

But now I can't ignore him much longer. His mumbling is getting louder and aimed more in my direction. He actually might be rapping, his hands are making lots of wild gestures and sometimes hitting my arm.

"Alright bruv?" he asks me. "I got some skunk in my pocket, you want some? I'll give ya a good deal."

"No, you're alright." I politely tell him.

But he keeps on. "Just a couple of quid. You'll like it."

Now the other passengers around us are looking at us, judging us for doing a drug deal on their public bus. I notice an elderly woman look at me and then at him. She only gave him a small glance, but for me she reserves a full stare. After a time she turns back to her husband and seems to mutter something that sounds like, 'Why doesn't he tell him to piss off?' How can I though? Who knows what kind of reaction that'll spark? You hear about knife violence on buses and gun crime, and how does that happen? Probably by telling a drug dealer on a bus to piss off.

I keep turning away towards the window, pretending to not know he's there but his selling spot is getting louder and more forceful. Finally the end of my patience is reached and I get up and off the bus, two stops earlier than I need to. I look to see if another bus is coming but can only see dark clouds approaching in the sky. I turn and start to walk the rest of the way, my mind imagining me telling that boy to piss off.

I'm never forceful enough when I need to be. That lad on the bus was annoying me yet I never did anything about it, unless you count looking the other way and pretending not to hear him as doing something. Now I'm walking on the cold and wet streets while he's on the warm bus. I should've told him I didn't want his drugs nor to hear about them. And that his behaviour, selling drugs on buses, was no way to carry on. Yeah, that's what I would've told him. I can see it now in my head. I'm looking in his eyes and telling him with a stern voice, clear and to the point. And if he'd got aggressive I would've told him that fighting was no way to solve problems, especially if it's because someone doesn't like you selling drugs on the bus.

That's what I would've done.

Chapter Four

The train pulls up at the platform. I look around to see which carriage looks the emptiest, though I know they're all going to be pretty busy at this time in the evening. In the end I go to the carriage doors closest to where I'm already standing. I join about 7 or 8 other people in waiting for the doors to open. The doors do open and yet there seems to be a second row of doors, a row of passengers. They turn around to see me and my fellow would-be passengers waiting for some space to be created so that we can go home too. I'm hit by a wind of sighs and groans before a sound of rustling newspapers being folded, briefcases being moved along the floor and polished black shoes making small steps away from the open door side of the train. There are now some gaps in the pack so we start to climb aboard.

Two men get on first and move towards the centre of the carriage to free up more space for the rest of us getting on. As do the next passengers and the next. It's my turn now and all I can see is a small gap to the left of centre.

The actual centre is taken up by two people who boarded before me. At the very left of the doorway is a man who's watched the episode unfold. He stands tall in a navy blue suit with tanned skin and gelled back dark hair. He wears his tie untied around his neck, his uniform outside of work I suppose, to show he can still look cool. And how cool does he look. I look down to the space where I must fit myself, and see his shiny, well-preserved shoes standing either side of a briefcase and a metre long umbrella. As soon as the doors opened he pulled his eyes away from his newspaper to give a look to the name of the station and then us on the platform. A look that seemed to say, 'What hellhole is this? What makes you think you're good enough to ride on this train with us?' Maybe his look didn't say that at all. Maybe there wasn't even a look. Maybe I was being too sensitive. Maybe I was imagining someone being angry with me for intruding on their calm journey home.

Now I'm stepping into the space available next to him. As I do this my left arm brushes against his newspaper which is spread out so far in front of him it looks like he's sharing it with the driver. Surely he'll bring the paper closer to himself so as to not obstruct anyone, namely me. I have a newspaper myself, in my right hand, rolled up, unread. I'm not going to open it up now to read, there's not enough space. The man in front's vision would be blocked and the man to my right would be tickled behind the ear by the corner of the paper. I'm not going to bother them just so I can read something that I'll know all about later. I don't even know the news headlines but that's fine, I only have a short train journey ahead of me.

If only the same thought would enter the head of my friend to my left. His paper has now been brought, or pushed, closer to his face. Not through his own doing it should be said. As the train is travelling I'm swaying left and right. Right, into the back of that passenger. And left, into the open newspaper of that passenger. A soft nudge with my elbow on the right and a brush on the newspaper with my shoulder on the left. There's a small rhythm. Two nudges and a brush. I'm just going with the flow of the train.

The rhythm is then joined by a sigh on about every second brush. This doesn't improve the rhythm and I want it to change. If it can't go back to the way it was before then I don't want any rhythm at all. I start to stand as still as possible, trying to glue my feet into the spot they're occupying on the floor. My eyes are fixed on the small section of the window I can see in front of me. I stop swaying from left to right but there's still a sigh. I notice that my left shoulder is now nestled underneath his newspaper. What can I do? If he doesn't want his precious newspaper to touch anyone or anything why doesn't he live in a bubble?

From my position now I get a glimpse of the headline on the front page of my friend's paper. It's something about cuts to the public services being made by the government to pay for the bailouts they gave to the banks. I doubt this man's affected much by it. He seems to be doing ok. He's probably one of the bankers or politicians who saw it all happen and then took home his salary and bonus at the end of it all.

The train starts to slow for a minute before eventually stopping. We are at a station. Not my station, that's the next one. The doors behind me open and I can see people in front of me trying to get off the train. I turn around and step off the train so as to create more room for those getting off. My friend watches us all stepping off the train. He looks like he's warning us off from ever stepping foot on his train again. Only that's exactly what I do. I stand beside the doors waiting for those to get off and then I hop back on. The man watches me like a hawk as I bother him yet again. After letting off those passengers there's now more room on the carriage than before. There's even a little space directly alongside my friend. "Excuse me." I say as I place myself next to him, my arm grazing against his newspaper. I press my back against the door and relax. This will be a smooth journey now. Any swaying from the train will be negated by the doors and there's a handle bar above my head if I need to hold on to anything.

Stood on the opposite side of my friend is another passenger who's peeking at my friend's newspaper. I look at the eyes of my friend and see them move to the left and notice this newspaper piracy. He begins to raise the left side of the paper in order to block any view of that page and to severely obstruct any view of the right side page.

I then watch his eyes even more closely. As he stands reading his newspaper, his eyes flick from the pages to the reader thief on the left, to me on the right and over the newspaper at anyone who is stood in front of him. And he sighs.

The train begins to slow down again; we're pulling into the final station. Everyone will be getting off and my friend will finally have to put his newspaper away. The passengers sitting get up and stay standing, there's nowhere to go while the train is still moving and the other passengers are stood in the aisles. Those stood around me turn to face me as it's on my side that the doors will be opening. My friend is one of these, and after folding his beloved newspaper, puts his arm behind my head. We look at each other. I try not to wonder what he's thinking this time. The train comes to a standstill and I turn around to wait for the doors to open. I look to my right in order to find the 'open' button, only to find my friend's fingers tapping away at it, almost in rhythm to his sighing. Maybe he doesn't realise that you can't step off the train whilst the train is still moving and the doors are closed.

Never mind, it's his problem. If he can only see around him things that concern him then what can I do? Sit him down and tell him he's not the most important man on this planet? Tell him that public transport is for everybody, not just snobs like him? No, what would be the point? He wouldn't understand my point of view. People like him only know the environment in which they inhabit. Anyone below their level of wealth and status is deemed unworthy of their time and respect. I decide to say nothing to him. I think that something somewhere at some time will poke this man in the face and tell him he's not the centre of the universe. I'm confident about that.

As is the way everybody steps off the train and turns right to walk towards the exit. I often feel like part of a herd when I do this. Everyone walks in the same direction, at the same pace, not speaking, not looking at each other, like a herd. Or an army. Often the passengers march to military precision in rows one behind the other. Left right, left right. But on this day there's nothing precise about my walk towards the exit.

You see, my steps are continuously being broken up by my friend from the train. He's walking whilst using his umbrella like a walking stick or those things hikers use. He's putting the umbrella down in front of him to the side when he puts one foot forward and then he leaves it there when putting the other foot forward. It's almost like he's walking with three legs. When I put my left foot in front there's no problem. But when I want to put down my right it's always obstructed by his umbrella. I can't complete a proper stride on my right side. I'm almost hopping on that side. And I can't pass because there are too many people in the crowd. It's just my luck that I'm walking directly behind this man and his three legs.

What can I do? I think about kicking the umbrella. That's the main obstacle and it would be less aggressive than kicking the man's legs. If he has a problem with it I could always say it was an accident, and it would have been. And if he has a go I can tell him that this is no place for carrying umbrellas in that way. With all these people around walking, you're asking for trouble.

And with that I kick his umbrella, and it is an accident. I wasn't looking where the bottom tip of the umbrella was landing nor where my foot was and so, yeah, they touched. What's he going to do? Is this it now, is everything going to spill over? All his anger at sharing his space on the train, his newspaper being touched by someone else and now his umbrella being nudged by a peasant. I have to be on guard here. Be prepared for him shouting at me or maybe attacking me with the umbrella. Be prepared, and have a counter in place. If he hits me with the umbrella, what will I do? Block and try to grab the umbrella or hit him myself? If he shouts at me, do I explain it was an accident or do I tell him to 'Piss off!'? Hopefully I won't need to do either; I don't feel like a confrontation right now after a hard day at work.

And it's not a confrontation I'm going to have either. He hasn't turned around or made any sort of gesture towards me. That's ok, got away with that one. All he did was lift the umbrella from the ground and hold it so that one end was sticking out in front of him and the other end behind him, into me, into an area significantly above my foot.

This is typical of London. People trying to sell drugs on buses, people not knowing how to behave in public. Strangers suspicious of each other, all exchanges of manners and respect out of the window. And it's getting worse. Children are being raised in this environment and are doing as they see. A rude, impolite, disrespectful cycle is forming.

I always try to tell myself that things don't matter, that things will change, that these people will get theirs, but they don't and here I am again, faced with more trouble. And what can be done about it?

What can I do about it? I feel useless in situations like on the bus. I imagine what I would've done afterwards but at the time I do nothing, just wait for the problem to disappear. Anyway, what can I do about it? I'm just one person. I can't influence the whole of society.

But then it always nags me that everyone thinks like that and that nothing will ever change if no one does anything. Nothing will ever change if I do nothing. I can't affect everyone but I can affect the next person and the next and hope that some kind of change will take place. Be the change you want to see in the world, that's how it goes. I could do that. I could be a Superman for society.

Chapter Five

I've spent the afternoon at the pub watching football on the telly. I stayed for a couple of drinks afterwards but it felt like time to go. I'm quite tired and I don't want a hangover tomorrow. I'm not drunk, just a little tipsy; I think that's the word for it. Whilst walking I can't help staring down at my feet, watching how they're not moving straight forward, just a little wonkily left and right. I wonder how the trail would look if I had paint underneath my shoes.

Michaela, my girlfriend of two years, is with me. She enjoys my behaviour when I've had something to drink. She finds it entertaining in an eccentric way. Not that she doesn't like me when I'm sober; she likes me all the time. She loves me. I doubt she believes the sun shines out of my backside, but she probably thinks there's light down there. In any case she often tells me how cute my backside is. It's great to have someone beside you who compliments your body, laughs at your jokes and applauds your surreal behaviour.

At the moment we're observing a comfortable silence, we spoke while we were out, we'll speak when we get home but we don't need to speak all the time. And as far as I know, we both feel like that.

As it has during the whole night, my mind is wandering around this idea I've had of being able to weed out the bad elements of society. So far I've had very little success, but that's ok, I doubt Superman was able to master all his talents at the beginning (he must've flown through a couple of ceilings whilst learning to fly, and I'm sure he burned holes in some walls when he found out he could fire out those hot beams from his eyes). There's been the cyclist who, after riding on the pavement, then pulled into the road and tried to pass through the red light. I stood in front of him to block his passing. Then there was the lad who dropped his litter on the street. 'I think you dropped something.' I told him. He didn't say anything in reply, only raising a finger to demonstrate his opinion. There was also an occasion with a bag thief in a coffee shop. I noticed a man sitting at a table, tying his shoelace. Or at least pretending to. He was actually reaching over to grab a handbag from underneath the next table. From where I was sitting I managed to shout at him to stop and he ran away. These went ok but they haven't been great successes. I would've liked to have spoken to these people, to get a chance to hear why they did what they did and explain why it's no good to anyone. I stopped them on these occasions but they'll do it again, I've no doubt.

When I think back over the last few days I realise my most successful case was where I pacified the hooligan who wanted to beat me up. He stopped me on the street the other night whilst I was walking home. He kept shouting at me, something about giving him dirty looks a few nights previously. I had no idea what he was talking about and tried to walk past him but he kept blocking my escape, cornering off the curb and grabbing hold of my coat. Eventually he believed my ignorance and pondered the possibility of mistaken identity. I then tried to tell him the wrongs of threatening people because they've looked at you the wrong way. He seemed to understand, if not completely agree. It was then I found my escape from the situation a lot clearer than previously. The man was crying and staring at the ground as I calmly walked past him. It wasn't how Superman would've done it or any kind of superhero vigilante but in my own little way I'd done something.

I wonder where he is now. I really hope he's not trying to beat up someone else, someone who isn't as ideological or genteel as me, who gives back as hard as he gets, then all my good work would've been for nothing. Still, it's early days in my mission and no one else actually knows about it yet. At some point I'll have to start spreading the word, then people will know how to react in such situations.

I think about bringing it up with Michaela. I'm not worried about her reaction or her opinion of it, she's always understanding and supportive of things I do and ideas I have – no matter how different they may be. The main issue is how I bring it up with her. Maybe I should recount for her the events of the last few days. Or I could just blurt it all out. Yeah, I'm going to blurt it out and give her a monologue.

"Do you think it's possible to do anything about the people in the world who piss you off or do wrong? Do you think that if you reason with a criminal, that you explain that what they're doing is wrong, they'll realise that and abide by the law? You know, instead of beating them or castigating them."

She looks at me a little puzzled and doesn't seem to have completely got the gist. She answers with something about prison, that this is the positive function of criminals being sent to prison.

"Um, yeah. Hopefully someone shows them the right path. Some kind of mentor, like a therapist or a priest. That has to be a part of their rehab, doesn't it?"

"Yeah, that's true, but that's not what I meant. I meant before they go to prison. Even before they commit the crime."

She's looking at me puzzled again.

"Huh? What should you do before they commit the crime?"

"Talk to them. Ask them why they're doing it. Put them off before they do it. Convince them it's wrong."

"But why would you do that? It's dangerous for a start…"

"Of course it is," I interrupt "But nothing will happen if you convince him not to."

"What if someone shoots you or hits you or maybe stabs you while you're discussing it?"

"Well…"

I can't find an answer.

"Why don't you become a policeman? Or a lawyer?"

"We already have plenty of those and things are still bad. I'm talking about members of the public. It would send out a stronger statement if the people helped their own people. Things will never change if people don't do anything."

"Why don't you leave it to the government?"

"The government? They're too busy looking after themselves."

We now just sort of continue our walk, her still looking at me awaiting a response. Me, looking at the ground, almost wishing I'd never said anything at all.

Footsteps behind us begin to get louder and then seem to be running as they get closer to us. A head and a voice poke themselves between us.

"Sorry lads, don't mean to bother ya."

As I say, a head is poked between our two walking bodies, almost hovering in mid air between our shoulders. He's a little too close for liking and, whether you wish to help society or not, it's always wise in London to check and be vigilant that no one is robbing you from behind. As I look back I only see his hands down by his sides. I'm not too worried about my things; my wallet and phone are in my front pockets, as are my hands. He'll have to get them out first before stealing anything. I look over at Michaela. Everything belonging to her is in her handbag hanging from her right shoulder. 'Clutch it tightly.' I try to tell her telepathically. She's looking at the man, I don't know if she heard me.

"Don't mean to bother ya. Could ya lend me £5 to get home?"

That was direct, to the point. Usually you have to listen to a long story about why they need the money, what happened to the money they did have or something. But this one didn't bother with any of that.

"No, sorry. Can't help you."

"Come on, please, I just need ya to lend me £5. I lost my wallet and now I got no money to get home."

There's the story, just had to wait a little for it. It wasn't very imaginative though, not worth waiting for.

"No, I'm sorry," And I shake my head this time. "We don't have anything; we've spent everything tonight."

I'm determined to be cool and calm in front of Michaela, to show what I was talking about. I'm going to deal with this man rationally and diplomatically. He won't get any money from us, there'll be no violence and, best of all, we will not resolve it by running away. To be honest I don't even feel scared or threatened. I only have small change on me and I doubt he'll want my phone. It would be completely different if I had my ipod with me. My most cherished possession. Also, by looking and listening to the man I feel a little more secure. I hope I don't tempt fate when I say he doesn't look like the scariest person to ever ask me for money. He doesn't look much like a mugger. More like a begging mugger.

It's down to my confidence that I tell him, "What do you mean 'lend me £5'? Are you going to pay it back to me?" In my head I think of saying something about giving him my address to send me the money or us meeting in the same spot next week. I don't feel my confidence is enough to actually tell him that though.

"Ok, not lend. Can you give me £5?"

All this time Michaela and I are still walking towards the bus stop with our new friend following us.

At least he interrupted the break in our conversation. I look over to Michaela to see her expression, to get an impression of what she feels about what's going on. She's frowning and staring at the ground as she walks. I don't know what that means. Is she scared, angry, nervous, cool? It's often hard to tell with her. Sometimes I tell her she looks sad or angry when in fact she's not. She says something about not needing to smile broadly and jump up and down all the time. That's fair enough I suppose.

"Look, I'm trying to be nice about this and asking you for the money nicely but if I need to I'll just take it, alright?"

"You what?" I say the first words that I think of

"Not many people would be so nice in getting money off ya. I'll take it if I wanna."

Now's my chance I feel. This guy's just heated things a little and it's going to be me who's going to cool it back down again. I raise my voice just a little bit to sound forceful enough.

"You mean that you'll get violent? Because we won't give you any money, you'll hurt us? Doesn't that sound a little silly? Do you need it that much?"

He doesn't even seem to be listening. I almost get the impression that he only said that to scare us into giving him the money sooner.

"Anyway, I told you we don't have anything."

"Yeah? Show me. Empty out your pockets."

This reminds me of being in school when the big kids wanted my money and would tell me to jump up and down to prove I had no coins in my pockets. How ironic it is now, I've only got coins in my pockets now.

"Yeah? Look," I stop and empty my pockets and hold out the contents in front of his face. My phone is there for the taking, "I've got that much money, an oyster card and my phone."

He motions to us to start walking again.

"I don't even have £5 to give you. Even if I wanted to."

"What about her?"

This is tricky. I know Michaela has quite a bit of money on her. We're planning on going to the supermarket on our way home and have agreed that she'll pay for everything as she has cash with her and I need to go to the bank.

"She's got nothing either." I jump in before he makes her show him the contents of her bag. "I just bought everything for her." Quick thinking, I congratulate myself.

"So you've both got nothing? What about we go to a cash machine and use your cards?"

As begging/mugging tactics go, this is a good one.

"What about I drag you both to a cash machine and we get my money?"

He's starting to sound more threatening too but I'm getting fed up with it all now and want it to stop. I put on my louder voice again.

"Look, I've told you again and again we don't have any money to give you and now I've just shown what I do have. Unless you want the change in my pocket, I think you're wasting your time."

And as quickly as he'd arrived he's disappeared to the other side of the road. He seemed to sigh and storm off like an angry teenager. I look over to Michaela and smile. In my head I'm thinking, 'He's gone, it's over, we did it.' She doesn't look as happy.

We stop walking. The frown she's had for the past 10 minutes or so is now a scowl. What's wrong with her? I thought she'd be pleased.

"Was that it? Was that your big plan?" she asks

"W-wha…" I can't find the words. I don't know what to say. I'm not really sure what's going on.

"Why didn't you do something? He could have robbed us or hurt us and you would've just let it happen. You were too busy trying to become his friend or something."

I'm in a small state of shock to be honest. I thought she'd at least be relieved that we weren't robbed or hurt, but instead she's angry at me. Didn't I just prove that what I was talking about could work? I warned the guy off without fighting him and we survived without running away.

"Come on, say something."

"What do you want me to say?"

"Aaargh!" she lets out an angry kind of groan "Say something. Don't be so quiet. This guy could have done things to us and you were there to protect me and you did nothing. You behaved like it was a laugh."

"But wait a sec," I interrupt; I need to find out what's wrong here. "he didn't do anything. Nothing happened. He wanted money, I told him no and he left."

"Eventually he did. You should have warned him off sooner. You were too nice to him."

"But if I hadn't been then maybe he would've got more aggressive. And who knows if he had a knife or something on him..?"

"And what would you have done then?"

"What do you mean?"

"If he'd had a knife, what would you have done? Would you have tried talking to him then?"

"Erm, I don't know. It's hypothetical. Probably, yes."

"Because you're scared."

"What? I'm not scared. Scared of what?"

She looks me in the eyes, as if she really wants me to understand this.

"Scared that you'll get hurt. Scared that you'll get punched. Scared that someone will.." she pauses, trying to find the right word. What word is she going to say? "defeat you. That you won't be the top man."

The gloves are off, home truths are being told. She looks satisfied that she's told me that. Almost smug, she's waiting for me to deny it. I can't though. She's right. I know she's right. I'm not one of those men who are so stubborn that they deny any negative aspect of themselves and will shout at their woman to put her down and make themselves feel bigger and more important. That's not me. I'm not going to admit to her that she's right, but I'm not going to admit to her she's wrong either. But I am going to stand up for what I did to the mugger.

"Look," I say calmly, trying to hide our conversation from the people passing us on the street. "I thought that was the best way to handle the situation. I don't think me starting a fight would have helped. Speaking to him and explaining the situation worked out much better in the end."

"Ooh, you could be like Jesus." she says enthusiastically. Luckily I know sarcasm when I hear it. "You could hang around at night when all the criminals are out, stand behind their shoulders and show them the errors of their ways."

'Not Jesus,' I think to myself 'Superman.'

"You're not Jesus, you're a wimp. A scared wimp who's afraid to get hurt, who's afraid to defend his girlfriend." Her voice is intensifying, she means this, she's not holding back. "You slag people off behind their backs and the minute they confront you, you quiver and hide. Don't you? I've seen it before. This was just another example."

Everything I've ever buried deep inside of myself in order to cope with each day, so as not to be reminded of my flaws and fears, is being dug up in front of me by someone I wanted to hide it all from the most. The one person I most wanted to see the good things in me, the positive side. Not this thing stood in front of her now being ripped to shreds.

"A woman needs a man who'll defend her and protect her. Even if you end up with cuts and bruises, at least you'd have done something. Not just been this weak and passive boy I've seen tonight."

I wait for some sort of reassurance from her. Something that tells me, 'but that's ok, that's who you are, I still love you.' She doesn't have to say anything; she could just smile or touch my arm. Or even just take away this angry expression and tone she's got right now.

I don't get it though.

"I.." she looks down to the ground "I need to be away from you right now. I need some space."

I say nothing. I barely do anything. I don't actually think I've moved a muscle for the last few minutes.

She turns and walks up the street. I stay where I am, my eyes watching her as far as they can see. I wait for her to turn around, just to give me a glance to say that everything's ok, or at least it's going to be. She doesn't though. Not once. Not even when she gets to the crossing at the top of the road and has to look back this way to check for any cars coming. I feel like I'm going to be sick.

Chapter Six

I switch off the TV. There's not a lot that's more depressing than watching crap TV in order to try and distract your mind from your problems. I'd managed adequately with watching a few things; even though today's events were clawing away at me I didn't feel as hollow and empty as I do now. I keep thinking whether Michaela has always felt like that and I was too blind to see it. The switching off of the telly has left an absence of sound, of noise. Now I can hear the silence. Every deafening chime of it. What am I going to do? I don't feel like I could sleep. Maybe I should have a drink. That would make me feel better, no doubt. It wouldn't be a good way to handle things though, would it? Who cares? Nobody. My one person in the world doesn't care; she ignores me and looks down on me now. There's some vodka in the freezer, let's mix that with some apple juice. I want to at least enjoy drowning my sorrows.

It's warm in here tonight. I don't really want to open the window. At this time of night all sorts of things will fly and crawl in. I'll leave it closed and take off my top instead. That feels better. Until,

Until I catch a glimpse of myself in the mirror. I take a step towards it to get a better look at this man. I want to see what this wimp looks like. I start with the face. It's not fat, that's not bad. It's pale though, almost always has been. It's quite dark around the eyes and when I point my face down I can see some heavy dark lines underneath them. I could easily be cast as a vampire. I look like a corpse with a bad haircut.

I look at my body. It's the body of a wimp. She's right. I'm afraid of getting hurt. And I would get hurt if I put this body into combat against another. I'm not thinking against some muscle man/Schwarzenegger type, but against a normal built bloke, I'd get walloped. Though today it was her words that hurt me.
There are no visible muscles, just skin. You can see the bones in my ribs. When I lift my arms you can definitely see them. My shoulders look like how a girl's would and my arms too. I tense up my right arm to see

how it looks. That makes it worse I think. I can now see just how small that bicep muscle is. Some people have ones twice or three times bigger than these. Pathetic. No wonder she's gone off. She doesn't need someone like me around her. Look at me. I look at the few strands of hair on my pale chest. They look like dirty weeds on barren unfertile land. Or dying flowers in a malnourished field.

I move closer to the mirror and press my forehead against it, closing my eyes, wishing to close them from my ever growing list of troubles. I stand still, eyes sewed shut, my mind drained of all thought, an inner calm within my grasp. Except for the distraction of that sound I can hear lurking behind me stabbing my concentration in the back. I don't need to look around to know what it is. It's the same dripping sound my broken tap always makes. Drip! If I keep my eyes closed it won't bother me. Drip! If I put my fingers in my ears I won't hear it. Drip! How am I going to sleep with that noise?! Drip! Maybe I should invite the landlord to try sleeping through it. Maybe that will get him to fix it. Two months of asking hasn't worked.

I open my eyes and immediately see them look back at me, my forehead still leaning against the mirror. I take a step back to gain better focus and stare into the reflection of my eyes. They say the eyes are the windows to the soul. I don't know if that's true. I can only see white framed blue stained glass windows, glass that could shatter at any moment. Michaela used to say they were what she liked most about me, but then again she said she liked many things about me.

I groan. I feel so sad. I just feel an ache inside of me and this vodka isn't helping. I cling to the belief that tomorrow is another day, possibly a different day. Whenever I've been down before that's often been the hope that's helped me. It might be my only hope this time. I lie on my bed and stare at the ceiling, trying to clear my mind free of its pain. It's not working. The ceiling's in shade, a dull and dark grey, its luminous and hopeful white gone, for today at least. I'm going to close my eyes. Tomorrow will come quicker that way.

Chapter Seven

And now the morning has come. I think I slept through the night without waking up. In any case I didn't lay for hours with my mind repeating what had happened earlier. And I fell asleep quite quickly after going to bed. After a few minutes I felt myself shake, as I normally do when my body switches off for the night.

First thing's first – coffee. I'll prepare that and it can cook on the stove while I go to the toilet, the second most important thing. Physically I feel good this morning. I've got no bad after effects from the vodka I had last night, if anything it's done me good. I feel energised, inspired, enthusiastic, ready for the world. Maybe I'm still drunk. Who cares? If it feels this good, let it continue.

I can feel the coffee kicking in now too. That's waking me up. Like being hit by a church bell. Give it to me. It's going to be a good day today, I can feel it.

I look out of the window. There are people walking, cars and buses moving. A lot of noise, a lot of activity. I look around for something else to occupy me while I finish my coffee. I see the mirror. The same mirror that mocked me last night, only today it's a little more sheepish, it doesn't seem to have as much to say. I stare at it, I listen intently for it to tell me something. I hear nothing. That's right; this mirror's got nothing to tell me today. Today it is I who is king. I look at my nude body. This is real, this is naked and raw. What you see is skin but what I feel is blood boiling and juices overflowing. Everything mixing and potions being formed inside.

Mmmm, nothing can stop me today.

Chapter Eight

Right, on my way to work again. Today's an early start so I'll get the train, it'll get me there quicker. I have to walk down that poncey street to get to the station. It's full of fancy delicatessens and gourmet pubs and clothes shops where you have to ring the bell to get in. At least they won't be open at this time of the morning. But there'll be plenty of the people who go to them. And I'll be sharing a train with them.

I'm almost at the station now, I'm just approaching it. There are quite a lot of people outside. It's not a school trip, is it? That's all I need, a train full of toffs, snobs and their little brats.

Here's the lad who's going to try to give me his free newspaper. I would take it to make him feel better but the paper's rubbish. It's all about City stuff and stocks. They know a lot of people will take it because it's free, but why? What do they want people to know that's so important? Do they give out a paper without charge just so people can save money? Or do they do it because it's easy access into people's minds? And eventually their wallets. This paper's always full of stock lists and adverts for different businesses attracting and inviting people to join the game. If it was a decent paper it'd be alright but when he's handing out that crap he's just in the way. And he's actually standing in front of the gate. What's he doing that for? Has his boss told him he's not giving out enough? They always look so upset and disappointed when I refuse their paper. Maybe they have to hand out all of them before they're allowed to go home. Now we have to take one of his rags before we're even allowed to get on the train. "Get out the way." I tell him as I walk through his one arm handing me the paper and the other holding the rest. I might not have said it as politely as that. Never mind, he should be thankful his pile of papers weren't hitting him like a boxing glove.

I managed to get a peek at the front page as I passed. It described 'the public's outrage at government cuts'. I suppose that means the public's angry at the mess the government's landed us in. Sure, everyone's angry and complaining, but no one's doing anything about it, are they? Typical. Moan, moan, moan, and do nothing and wait for the next problem to moan about.

I pass through the gate and into the tunnel towards the stairs which will take me up to the platform. Why are there so many here today? There's a crowd gathered at the bottom of the stairs, what's all this about? They don't seem to be doing anything or going anywhere. I think they're doing that 'after you, ladies first' nonsense. I'm not having anything to do with this. I'm going to walk through the lot of them. I don't care whose shoulders get nudged nor who feels my elbow in their ribs.

I finally make it up to the platform, just in time to see the train arrive. The platform's busy, as is the train. I'm getting on this one though. No matter what. I move myself to the front of the waiting passengers. The doors open and I see men blocking the door way. Those who had their backs pressed against the doors which have just opened turn to us, to mock us. I see them looking down on us. I can see in their eyes, 'There's no room for you here. Get the next train'. The men on the platform blow their whistles, we have to hurry, the train's getting ready to leave. A man next to me, a real bright spark, bangs on the side window, "Can you move down please?" he cries to those standing in the aisles. I have a better idea. As the whistle is blown again to warn the doors are closing, I grab the tie of the man closest to me and pull him from the train down to the platform. I then quickly jump on to the train before the doors manage to close shut.

I catch the expression of the man who so kindly gave me his place on the train. He doesn't know what him. He'll think again the next time he looks at me like that. As the train sets off I wink at him and blow him a kiss. At least he's got his free newspaper to read while he waits for the next train.

Chapter Nine

It's been a tough day at work. Everyone seemed to be giving me lip, showing me no respect whatsoever. I work as a waiter in a restaurant in the heart of London. It's an alright job, it pays ok and I have fun with those who work there. It's not a job I want for the rest of my life but it'll do for now, until I have a clearer idea of what job I would like for the rest of my life. But there are times when it doesn't feel worth the hassle that customers give me. I'm often spoken to rudely, or at least impolitely. They don't usually look at me and when they do, it's with disdain through rolled eyes. There was this one stuck-up posh girl today who talked to me like I was a piece of dirty chewing gum stuck to the bottom of her shoe. She thought she was a right princess. I put her in her place though. I made her feel so small that she would've needed to look up to a grasshopper. Fair play to her though, she didn't cry. I'll give her credit for that. She might've cried after she'd run off. Maybe she sobbed in the toilets with her mates, telling them what an arsehole I'd been to her. Telling them all sorts of cobblers so she could get some sympathy while they brush her hair and feed her grapes. I hate these kinds of girls. They stroll around like they own the place and everyone in it and then when you try to bring them in line with reality they start crying and pretend to be the victim. They're too used to getting their own way all of the time, they've never been told 'No' before.

Unfortunately in my neck of the woods there are a lot of these sorts about. I can see a few of them now in the train carriage with me, shouting in their mobile phones, 'Do this, do that!' I bet if the person on the other end told them, 'No. Get stuffed!' then we'd see the waterworks come and the whiny voice crying, 'He was so mean to me. It came from nowhere. I'm always so nice to him and now he's calling me a bitch.'

Part of me (the lower part) can understand some women for being tough and demanding of people. These women being the beautiful elite. If a woman is beautiful with everything looking perfect and in the right place then she can talk to me or any man however she likes because at the end of the day if a man gets what he wants from her then he's going to enjoy it.

Sadly there are no women like that around me today. There's only one who'd be worth a night of my time and even then I'd need a lot to drink and some good lighting. I think I might as well take advantage of Michaela being gone. For the time being at least I'm a bachelor and we all know what that means. There'll be no more watching 'Countdown' while I eat my dinner or listening to stories about Primark sales or endlessly watching her try on subtly different dresses.

Anyway, it's been a tough day at work but it's over now. I'm on my way home to put my feet up. One more stop and I'll be there.

I'm trying to keep myself awake. It's been a relaxing journey home, I've had two seats to myself the whole time, and my eyes have shut a couple of times.

Something tells me that's not going to happen again though. To be more specific, an oaf has just planted his big wide self next to me. His legs and feet (that's what I think they are, I haven't looked down, they might be skis) are so long and crammed into the tight legroom of the train that they're spilling into my side of the two-seater. I'm slowly getting squashed against the window, like those things that squash abandoned cars. He's a City slicker by the looks of him, a banker or a trader or something. I say that because he's wearing a pin-stripe suit and looking around the bus like it's a punishment to be so close to the peasantry. He might not work in the City of course, it's just that in my experience people like that usually do.

"Do you think you could move along a little bit? To give me some more room." he asks me.

Is he taking the mick? His newspaper lies so far on my lap that I can also read what he's reading. It seems that the MP's have been dipping their fingers into the tills again. Overspending their expenses accounts on such diverse requisites as turrets on their homes and chauffeur driven cars for 100 metre journeys. And it's the defenceless taxpaying public like me who's paying for it all. It'd be bad enough at any time, not least now when the economy's in pieces and 1000's are losing their jobs.

"I can't really go much further," I tell him. "Why don't you stretch your legs out in the aisle?"

"But then I'll intrude on the space of this young lady." and he looks up at this woman who's standing beside the seats on the opposite side of the aisle from us. I think 'young lady' was pushing it. 'Young' definitely not, and 'lady', well, judging by the looks she's giving me, I doubt very much.

"Of course ideally you'd give up your seat for an elderly gentleman like myself. A young lad like you shouldn't have too much difficulty in standing on the train for a bit."

"No." I say, not agreeing with him, just going along with it.

But then his tone changes.

"Go on boy, show a little respect. Get off your lazy arse and do something for someone else for a change."

He's definitely taking the mick. Who does he think he is? He can't just come on here and boss me around.

"What? What did you say?" I think maybe I hadn't heard correctly and I'll give him a chance to say what he really means.

Then he turns to me and looks sympathetically at my face, like he's talking to a small child who's being corrected for using the wrong grammar.

"Come on, let these seats be taken by people who've done a days work, not by layabouts like you."

47

It seems that now the man and me have the attention of this part of the train carriage. After his last sentence he turned to some of the gazing faces fixed on us, smugly rejoicing in mutual appreciation. I'm being bullied by toffs. I'm not having this.

"Who are you calling a layabout? I've been to work today as well." I turn in my seat to face him.

"Oh really? And where is it that you work if I may ask?"

"I work in a café."

He grins like he'd made a bet with himself on what I was going to say.

"Maybe that's not an as important job as yours, but it's still a job."

He opens his mouth, ready to say something, his face still smug. I don't give him the chance.

"I work very hard for a living. I started at 7.30 this morning and was on my feet for the whole day except for my 30 minutes lunch break. What about you? How long have you been on your feet today? Huh? How much do you deserve to sit here now? You've been sitting for most of the day, haven't you?"

His face doesn't look so smug any more. He looks shocked and baffled that someone's come back at him. He looks like he'd like to say something but doesn't have a clue what. I'm not going to give him the chance anyway. I'm enjoying this.

"And I bet it was your secretary who did most of the work, wasn't it? Running here and there. Getting you this and that."

I look around the carriage. No one seems to be looking at us any more. Suddenly the view out of the window and the pattern in the carpet are more fascinating. The same for the man next to me. I turn back in my seat to face forwards. I'm still hunched up next to the window though.

"Do you mind? You're coming over into my side of the seat."

He doesn't even look at me. He only manages to glance over at where his right leg is and how much space I'm sitting in. Then he shifts in his seat and puts his left leg in the aisle.

The train's pulling in to my station. It would've been nice to stay a little longer to bask in the glow of satisfaction but I don't fancy getting another train back.

"There's a good boy," I tell him "Now excuse me, this is my stop."

I get up and manoeuvre myself past my new friend and weave through the bodies standing in the aisle. They're all staring at me. All I did was speak my mind. I know, in England that's strange and people usually stare at you when you do it.

I now stand on the platform satisfied with how the situation ended. Just because Michaela doesn't like my idea of helping society doesn't mean I'm going to forget about it. If anything I'm more positive about it than ever after what's happened today. I feel everyone's been put in their place. I feel I'm beginning to be the change I want to see in the world. I only feel bothered that any of it's happened in the first place. What's wrong with these people? What makes them think they can run the show and treat me like a fool?

Like this woman waving her finger at me, directing me to come to her like a schoolteacher does to a naughty infant. Why is she doing it to me? I can see beside her a large suitcase; she probably wants me to carry it down the stairs for her. Yeah, I'll do that. It's good to do things for others, and I do plenty. Wait a second, she's already started to walk down the stairs. Maybe it's not her suitcase. What's up with her? I reach the top of the stairs and she turns and says to me, "Will you bring that down for me?" She turns again and continues walking. 'Please would've been nice.' I think to myself. At least she didn't call me Jeeves or Boy or whatever her normal slave's name is.

She reaches the bottom before me and stands impatiently with her hands on her hips looking up at me. When I'm two steps from the bottom she says to me, "You can leave it there." and points to the ground beside her. She doesn't look at me. I don't throw the case down but I do let it drop a little.

"You don't have to slam it, do you? I hope for your sake nothing's broken."

And with that she lifts the handle and walks towards the exit, pulling the case behind her.

"You're welcome." I mutter

"Welcome for what?" she stops and turns to me, "For damaging the goods in my case? I think not."

"You'll be lucky to get thanks for that, mate." a third voice says, that of the station guard "I wouldn't thank you for throwing my things down like that."

I don't feel like arguing with the woman as one confrontation with an elderly person on the train feels enough for today. But I'm not going to stay silent to this guard sticking his nose into my business.

"Luckily you don't have to."

This is a quiet station, with not many people coming through it, and the guards here are often looking for something to do. Even now as we're speaking he's sitting down next to the control box with a newspaper. If someone has a problem with the ticket gate he'll just press a button without getting up.

"Next time someone wants something carried down, I'll let you do it, shall I? As long as that's not too much work for you"

He smiles but he knows I'm right.

I follow the woman to the gate, gently nudging her case with my foot.

"And don't do that. That's not very nice, is it?"

"Why don't you keep your nose out and concentrate on your job? That crossword's not going to finish itself." I say as I walk through the gate and out of the station.

Chapter Ten

Tonight's going to be a few drinks with the people from work. Should be a laugh, at least it's a night out. I'm running a bit late so I'm rushing to the train station. I can see up ahead they've already brought halfway down the big rolling shutter thing. They always do that just before the last trains leave. Oh great, my mate from earlier is on duty. And he's not alone. He seems to be chatting up a lady person. Oooh, the perks of the job. I bet he's telling her, 'I'm not going to let you get on the train unless you give me your number.' Maybe the train's arrived because she's leaving him. Or more likely she's had enough of him. He's still smiling though, I think that's the best luck he's had with a girl for a while.

I approach the gate. He turns and sees me and we both acknowledge each other. I insert my ticket and the machine rejects it. The same happens again. And again.

"You having a problem?" he asks me. He's been watching the whole time and now he asks. He's bright this one.

But I need his help. What else can I do?

"Yeah, the machine won't accept my ticket."

"Alright, let's see what we can do. Put the ticket in."

I do. And it comes out again without the gates opening.

"Ok, put it in again."

Same result.

"Alright, and again."

He looks away from me and the machine to the wall beside us. He knows it's not going to open again this time either. He's got me under his thumb. Now he looks at me, smiling as he chews his gum.

"Did you give that girl this same level of customer care?"

He doesn't reply. He just keeps smiling and chewing at me smugly. Come on, say something. Give me something to fight against.

"Oh look, it's come out again. Let me see what I can do here." He goes over to his little electrical cupboard. I don't see what he does but the roller shutter thing closes completely and the ticket gate opens.

"You've got to know how to treat these old machines." he tells me, looking pleased with himself, "A little respect and TLC and they work fine."

"Is that what you gave that girl?" I say as I walk past him, then muttering, "Prick."

"Oi," I feel him grab me by the back of my shirt collar. I'm surprised and freeze a little, "Don't feel that you can waltz round 'ere with that chip on your shoulder without someone wanting to give you a slap. A little squirt like you shooting his mouth off don't matter to me, I see 'em everyday. And when you put the frighteners on 'em, they'll run home to their mummies."

I'm not a little squirt and what's this about a chip on my shoulder?

"Wha…" I try to wriggle free from his grip but he moves his hand up around the back of my neck. He's got a good hold of me, it actually hurts.

"No, don't move. You've got to stand still and listen to this, it'll do you good."

I feel now that I couldn't move even if I wanted to.

"It don't bother me what you do. I know a kid like you's going to get his comeuppance one way or another. But then when you go picking on old women like you did today and then you give me backchat, well, it makes me think maybe I should be the one to teach you. Hmm, what do you think?"

He squeezes his hand and brings his face closer to mine to see my grimace. Then he gives me one last big squeeze before pushing me away.

"I don't want to hear a peep from you when I see you in this station, you hear?" he warns me one last time before going back to his little cupboard thing.

I move my head from side to side and exercise my neck. It all feels better now he's let go. I can gather my thoughts now. Was that it? Is that all he's going to do? Some big warning? While he had me in that hold he could do what he liked, now I'm free I can give some back. I walk back towards him.

"Look at you, the fat controller. What are you going to do? Pull to the side everyone who comes in here that you don't like the look of? Like some cowboy."

I'm standing in front of him now and stick my face so close to his that I can see the hair growing in his nostrils.

"This isn't a bar or a club. This is a train station, people will do what they like and no jobsworth twat like you is going to do anything about it."

And with that as quick as a flash he's grabbed me by my t-shirt and pulled me on to the wall. My back slams against it and now, to go with his nostril hair, I'm close enough to see the patterns in the iris of his eyes. He's keeping me pinned against the wall with a firm grip of not only my t-shirt but also some of the skin on my chest.

"I tried to give you a chance, just a little warning, but no, you had to get all cocky, didn't you?"

His eyes are big and round now. His face has turned red. As he talks to me he's almost dribbling, like when a dog is inches away from a plate of meat.

How can I get out of this? A woman would probably knee him in the balls in this situation. I don't even think I could manage that, he's too close to me. There's no leverage to grab him and swing my knee into him.

"Do you wanna say something now? Huh? Cat got your tongue? Not so mouthy now, are you?"

What can I say? I'm not apologising if that's what he's after. I've done nothing wrong. I just need to get out of this position then I'll tell him something with my fist.

Hello, what's that I see? A video camera in the corner between the two walls and the ceiling. Is he going to risk his job by doing something to me? He'll probably get sacked when they see what he's already done, assaulting an innocent passenger.

"Look, there, the video camera, watching everything you do. You won't have a job tomorrow. It's a long way down from working in a train station."

Bang! His right knee comes crashing into my gut. I feel like there's no air to breathe. He knocked it all out of me and now I have no strength to take in any more. I can barely stand either. I'm letting him hold me up at this point. Bang! Again, the same shot. This time he lets go of me and now I'm down on my knees. I feel water coming out of my eyes. Not tears but just like he's hit some water inside of me and it had to be released somewhere. I suppose I made him angry about the camera. Maybe now he thinks that if he's going to lose his job he might as well go out with a bang. Shall I fight back? I think I can take him if I just manage to start breathing again. Maybe that wouldn't look good on the camera though. Maybe in court they'd use it against me.

Now he grabs my hair. Is he going to pull it and then scratch and pinch me like a girl? He grabs my hair and pulls me across the ground, then lifts my head and says, "Say hello to the camera. Say hello camera."

Has he gone nuts? Is he some psycho train station hooligan? What's he going to do next?

He still has hold of my hair when he brings his face towards mine.

"You see, you can say hello to that camera and I can punch you and no one is going to see it. You get it? All this is just between you and me."

What? Those cameras are just for show, just to scare people off from doing something? I'd always suspected it.

"When you had that problem with your ticket I thought you might want to kick off, so I prepared myself just in case. In that cupboard over there with all the buttons, I switched off the cameras."

It's quite clever when you think about it. I'm surprised he did though.

So now my option of taking the video tape to the police is gone, what do I do now? I'm in a bad predicament being held by my hair with my knees on the ground. Oh, there's one thing I can do without any trouble. Splash! I spit right in his face.

He grabs me tightly by the neck again and wipes his face with his sleeve.

"You know, the shame about this not being filmed is that I won't be able to watch it over again."

I just manage to take in the severity of what he says before his right hand whacks me in the face. My face is thrown over to the other side and I have no idea what to think. He pulls my face back towards him and hits me again. This time I somehow land on my side. I feel a tickling dripping feeling from my nose. I suppose it's blood.

I hear a loud noise coming from near my head. I can just about make out that it's the sound of the giant station door being opened. I now feel myself being pulled up from the ground and dragged towards it. The door opens from the bottom and right now it's open about half a metre. I'm thrown through the open section on to the street behind, like Indiana Jones if he'd been thrown.

I feel that I would like to stay on this pavement for a long time, or at least for tonight. My face hurts and my gut is sore but my pride is still defiant. I use my last strength to pull myself up and tell the guard this isn't over.

"This isn't over. I'll have you. You'll see."

He smiles and shakes his head as he lowers back down the door to the station. He might not believe it now but he'll get his. I'll have a plan for him. When he's least expecting it.

I think I'm going home now. My night out is pretty much over, I'm not in the mood now. I'll have a drink at home instead.

Like when walking home drunk I've still got my senses about me. I know the way home and I know I've got change in my pocket to stop at the off-licence at the end of the road. I'll just take out the change to count it all. My palm is filled with coins but I can't see them well. Nothing to do with me, it's the light; one of the streetlamps isn't working. I'm squinting when I hear footsteps approach me. Like a blind person I look in the direction of the sound but can't see what I'm looking at. The footsteps get closer and I can make out that it's two policemen.

"You alright young man?" one of them asks me.

"Aha, fine."

"Nothing you want to report?"

"Report? What do you mean?"

"Well your face is pretty bashed in…"

"Well spotted Columbo."

One of them seems to smile, the other looks intently at my bashed in face. There is more of me you know? Now I know how girls feel when men only look at their tits when talking to them. What do they want? Typical coppers, sticking their noses in where they're not wanted.

"Have you been assaulted? Do you want to come with us to the station and give us a description?"

"Are you two out on the pull? I'm not coming anywhere with you." They look at each other. They realise I'm on to them. Though that one's stopped smiling.

"Don't be cocky."

"Are you even policemen, or are you going to a YMCA concert? Eh, bent coppers, gives it a new meaning, doesn't it?"

"You watch what you say, son" says the other one and points at me

"Oh you've perked up. I thought you only spoke when he told you to. Like a ventriloquist's dummy. Or a gimp."

And he comes for me. He launches himself at me until he's stopped by his mate. I don't know if he's angry or if I've turned him on. His mate puts his arms in front of him, blocking him from me, saying something like, 'Leave him, leave him. He doesn't matter.'

"And what about you Columbo? Where's your dirty old raincoat? At home for later when you'll go flashing in the woods?"

"Ha ha ha" he smiles and laughs. He liked that one. The old ones are the best.

I can't tell you what happens next. The last thing I remember seeing clearly is his elbow flying towards me and hitting the bridge of my nose. Then I was lying on my back with everything fading in and out. I don't know if I dreamt this but I have a vision of the policemen arguing with each other. One shouting, 'What did you do that for?' And the other saying, 'It was retaliation. He hit you first!' And then maybe one punched the other in the face. That may or may not have happened. My memory from then is all a bit hazy and blurry.

Chapter Eleven

My eyes open and for a few moments I've got that feeling of not knowing where I am. I realise I'm at home and then realise I've got a headache. Am I drunk? Do I have a hangover? No, I got beaten up. Twice.

I wish I was hung-over, it'd be less embarrassing. I wish I was hunched over the bog with my guts spilling out. I'd feel better than I do now, with the pain of getting roughed up by a copper and someone who works at a train station.

I need to get over this quickly and plan my revenge. I'm not going to let them get away with this. I've got no idea right now but I will do. Good revenge takes time to organise.

I get out of bed to look at myself in the mirror, to inspect the damage. I've got bruises along my right side. Someone must've kicked me without me knowing. I don't feel much down there though, it all feels pretty normal. Probably not inside though if it's got that colour on the outside.

My face has got some marks and bruises on it too. It might be my blurry vision but I think my right side is slightly dented. Like a fist has left a print behind. And I know for a fact my nose didn't look like that yesterday. Jesus. I'm going to have a cup of coffee and a paracetemol.

I go back to the mirror. I've got to toughen my body up, make it a weapon in itself. If people see a big body and muscles then they know they'll have problems if they start with me. Even if it's just a statement to put people off from fighting me, or a statement to let them know their place. That's often all that's needed anyway. Do you ask a big fella to say sorry when he spills your drink in the pub? Do you tell him and his mates to shut up when they're being loud outside your flat? Even though you're trying to sleep. What if a man in a vest showing off his muscles and tattoos is taking up two seats on the bus, do you ask him to move? Do you sit on the edge of one of the seats? Or do you sit somewhere else? It's like advertising. The slogan's saying, 'Don't mess with me, it will hurt!' And even if a fight does break out, I'll have more power to deal with them.

I just need to get this body from somewhere. I take out two cans of baked beans from the cupboard. For a start I'll use these as weights, very light 250g weights. I have one in each hand down by my side and lift them up above my head. Then down again. And up. I do this for a few minutes until I think that I should do other exercises too. I stretch my arms out as far as I can then bring them back in to my chest. Out. Then in again.

It's going to take too long though at this rate. I'm going to need a little help. There's a fitness shop in the shopping centre, I'll go there and get a few things.

Chapter Twelve

It's been a few weeks since I went to the fitness shop. A few weeks spent alone in my flat like a warrior in exile waiting and preparing to be launched into battle again. It was a very fruitful visit I made to that fitness shop. I bought some dumbbells and some of those powder drink things that let you gain weight. And a little extra product from the manager.

After telling him about my desire to quickly gain a muscular body he showed me some products which weren't for sale on the shelves of the shop. He sold me some pills which he said would give me the muscles and physique I required in next to no time. And as I seemed a nice lad he gave me a good price for them, though he also said as long as I don't tell anyone and that I would go back to him for more in the future.

I'll have to go back there today as I finished off the remainder last night before going to bed. I've bulked up since I started taking them but not as much or as quickly as I'd like. So last night I swallowed all that was left in the jar to speed things up a bit. It was more than the man said I should but what harm can it do? All it'll do is work faster.

It seems that this small skinny body, the body of a wimp as my girlfriend put it, has got some life left in it yet. Last week I arranged to play some football with some lads, one of which I'd gone to school with. Adam his name was. He always had what you might call a fiery temper, which seemed to be sparked off in the most unnecessary situations. For example I remember a time when he began to shout at me because we disagreed on the age of Ian Wright who was playing for Arsenal at the time. I can vividly see his face in my memory, almost spitting from his mouth in anger as he shouted at me in disagreement. "NO HE'S NOT THAT AGE!!" I think I remember someone holding him down in his seat, to stop him from lunging at me. I just ignored him. I agreed to disagree. I wasn't going to get so angry over such a small thing.

It was quite typical of him though. There were several episodes of him getting very angry at such small annoyances. I think maybe he believed himself to be better than everyone and never ever in the wrong. And his way of displaying this was to hysterically shout at them, in some way to prove that he who shouts loudest wins.

Or something.

So I was a little intrigued to see how he was nowadays, almost 15 years later. Had he matured at all?

The two of us said hello and acknowledged each other. We didn't chat and catch up on old times. My friends in the group didn't really know him and I didn't know the two boys he was mostly talking to. He didn't look too happy to be there to be honest. There seemed to be a scowl fixed onto his face.

We divided ourselves up into two teams with me and Adam on opposite sides. This didn't matter too much to me. Being on the same team wasn't going to help too much if he still had the anger issues he had as a kid. I remember us playing a match for our school team when he went mad at me for throwing the ball back to our goalkeeper. "WHAT ARE YOU DOING THAT FOR?" I remember him shouting. Not even our manager/teacher Mr Richardson said anything to him, probably in fear.

This game was good, I enjoyed it. It was mostly light hearted. There was a lot of banter, the boys showing off their skills, trying to score spectacular goals.

The mood changed in one single moment though. Adam had the ball in midfield and I took it from him, accidentally knocking Adam to the ground as well. I then had possession of the ball, or so I thought. Just as I was about to pass the ball to a team mate I felt a large kick take out my standing leg from under me. I was down. My first feeling was of surprise. I'd never been fouled like that in a game before. Especially in a friendly kickabout like this. But that foul was like in a professional game, it merited a yellow card.

"WHY ARE YOU FUCKIN KICKIN ME FOR YOU IDIOT?" screamed Adam leaning over me, his face looking the same as it did all those years ago. Some of the boys pulled him away. They held him back like a dog owner does when their dog barks uncontrollably at another dog.

"Hey, calm down. Take it easy." one of them said.

I was still surprised. Now I sat there wiping off some of the mud that was on me. I couldn't believe this was happening again.

"Looked like a fair tackle to me." I heard someone say. And I didn't hear any one disagree.

"Yeah but Adam's not used to getting tackled by crap players like me, is he? He doesn't like it."

"YOU SHUT UP!" he barked at me, trying to wrestle himself free.

"He wants a red carpet in front of the goal. And anyone who stops him gets what I got." I stood up and wiped off the biggest blob of mud from my hands.

"Let him go." I told his keepers, "Let him go. Let's see what he's got to say."

I moved my hands to say 'come here'.

Adam was set free and came straight towards me, his face full of lines of emotion and his eyes squinting with anger. I didn't feel threatened; I knew he was only going to shout at me. He had that familiar pose where he stood and leaned forward with his face. Or in fact his mouth. It was like his mouth was his weapon. And it was going to defeat me. I couldn't outshout him. Especially as I had nothing to argue about for I'd done nothing wrong. Plus, he looked like a prat in front of everybody and they could all see he was in the wrong.

So, was I just going to stand there and let him scream at me? No. I had a much better plan.

He approached me in what felt like slow motion. He was already shouting at me but I wasn't listening. The closer he got the more excited I got. I could feel the excitement gathering like a storm inside me. I felt boundless energy boiling in my veins. I could feel my eyes lighting up as they fixed themselves on the prey. My mouth felt like it was slobbering like a dog studying a plate of meat. My meat, my prey was within distance now. I clenched my right fist and felt the surge of power run through my arm. In the next second I was going to explode. Anger and frustration were going to pour out of me like lava. I was ready. I was going to enjoy this.

I felt so free and able. On top of the world. It felt like nothing could stop me. I put, what felt like my complete body weight, into my right fist and I threw it towards his face. I felt great; this was going to hurt so much. I couldn't wait to see it connect and assess the damage. I could feel myself licking my lips.

'Pow!' My fist landed across his mouth and jaw. It was a beautiful clean punch. Boxers would've been proud. And the sound it made when it hit him, wonderful! A wonderful thud! His face and head swung over to the other side and started swaying like those dog ornament things.

A hush came over everybody. No one knew what to say or do. That was just fine, I was saying and doing enough for everybody. I felt something sharp catch my fist. I hoped it was his tooth.

Then I grabbed him by the front of his t-shirt, stood him up straight and threw my knee into his midriff. And again. I didn't feel my knee hitting much, there was no bone there like in his jaw to tell me the impact it was having. When I punched his jaw there was that lovely crashing thud sound. Now there was nothing. Just Adam hunching himself over my knee, trying to defy my attempts to keep him on his feet. That told me something about the impact. I thought about his organs and muscles inside and the impact on them. They must have thought it was the Blitz. I wanted to know what that looked like.

While he was still holding on to my leg I took advantage of the right side of his face that was visible to me and I swung my right elbow into his cheek. That didn't make a sound either. I thought I should maybe do it again. But then he was falling to the ground. I moved quickly to catch his fall and gave him one last punch as a send off.

He dropped to the ground in a heap and seemed to fall asleep. Then everyone stepped in to pull me away but it was fine, I'd had enough.

I saw him lying there. Around his nose and mouth was smeared in blood. This was the greatest memory I would take from there that day, that memory of seeing him lying there powerless to what I'd done. That powerful feeling that I had, that I felt almost unstoppable would pass, that much I knew. It was like a drug high or an orgasm, it wouldn't last forever. But what I saw in front of me will. The next time I'm faced with a challenge, someone who doesn't know how to behave or show respect, I'll remember that feeling and summon it again to help me.

Aaah, and then I wanted more. I needed to burn off more of that energy. I wondered if I should I fight again? The other lads were backing off from me. They didn't look like they wanted anything to do with me. I left them with the patient, let them clean him up. I jumped over the park fence on to the street outside. Where would I go? I thought I should go find Michaela, tell her what her wimpy boyfriend's just done, let her lick the blood off my knuckles. I needed something to fight against, some pain to urge me on. Something like her nails clawing at my back, my sweat pouring into the marks and stinging. But where was she? She knew where I was. She could get in touch if she wanted. I didn't need to rely on her to get what I wanted.

That was a week or so ago and now my confidence is higher, my tail is definitely up.
I lie in bed now thinking about it. I've just dished out a beating to a bad memory from growing up. This was one person who didn't show me any respect then or now and needed to be taught a lesson. He'll think again next time he considers himself above being tackled on a football pitch.

And the others who were there too. They didn't think I was capable of something like that. That I was too weak, too scared and too nice. But now they've seen there's a line and when that line's crossed, I'm ready.

I'm slowly teaching people respect. Eventually I'll change society. Of course someone's going to tell me it's not how Superman did it, that he wasn't so violent. That's rubbish. Admittedly, he rescued people from fires and natural disasters, caught people falling from buildings, I think he turned back time once because he didn't know what else to do. That's all fine, I'm not going to do any of that. But when the bad guys came looking for him, what did he do? He fought them, beat them up and destroyed the city too. If I have to do the same to succeed...

Now it's time to see what impact these pills are having.

I step out of bed and walk over to the mirror to look for any change. This is now a firm part of my daily routine. The first thing after getting out of bed is to look at my body in the mirror and measure it with the tape measure. I can't see the tape measure anywhere but I can see a difference in my body since yesterday. Everything seems much bigger. My chest, my shoulders, my arms. My six-pack too.

I feel every muscle on my body. It's not so much that I feel stronger, more that I have greater protection now. Before my body was like a near bare chicken wing. You'd need to nibble the bone to get your money's worth of meat. Now there's plenty to go round. The colonel should think about charging extra.

I look at my arm, how much it's grown. The muscle has been reinforced like an army recruiting more men.

Time to get dressed and go outside. I want to see what this body can do.

Chapter Thirteen

I approach the door and that familiar smell hits me. You just don't get it in any other place that sells alcohol – a trendy bar, a skanky bar, an off-licence. Even an alcoholic's bedsit doesn't have that pub smell. I've arrived at my local now to watch some football on the telly. It's pretty packed. I don't know if there'll be any room for me to stand and get a good view. I'll try anyway; it's a game I'd rather not miss. I know *they* always tell you that but for me tonight, that's true. Because I don't want to miss it, not because *they* say I don't want to miss it. The pub looks a lot smaller with so many people in it. I can't see any room at the bar, nor near the screen. There's not a lot left of the game. I've got 1½ eyes fixed on it whilst I'm looking for a spot to station myself. I'll miss the end if I go looking for another pub. I'll stay. I'll sneak in a space somewhere. Maybe there's a young lady I can squeeze next to.

I manage to get close enough to the bar to order my pint. Around the bar are two rows of men locked together forming a human wall, except for the small gap I made to get my drink. This might be the best I can do. I'm near the bar and I can see the telly. It's a little claustrophobic but it looks like everywhere is. Now I can give the game my undivided attention.

72

I've needed this after the day I've had. This is a relaxing night-in for me. Today has been anything but relaxing. It's not been hard-work or stressful but there's just been a lot to do.

It began with me leaving my flat after discovering my extra weight. I went out for a run but when I got to the zebra crossing by the park I had a little problem with a driver. This man stopped to let me cross and so I started to when he started tooting his horn at me. At first I didn't know what to think. Maybe he knew me. Maybe he didn't mean to do it. But then he wound down his window and shouted at me, telling me to hurry up. I stopped and turned to him. I told him I can take as long as I want and he's not the king of the road. Then he turned the air blue, telling me 'Get out the fuckin way!' So I went over to his window and told him I had the right to cross the road and he should stop being a dick. It was then he tried to grab me from his seat. You know like when a little kid runs past you and you pretend to try and grab it, it was like that. Of course he couldn't catch me. He was too restrained by the seatbelt and lack of space. I could see him getting more and more frustrated. Now it was like he was the kid trying to grab the adult. He got even more frustrated when I started slapping him as well. Every time I dodged one of his grabbing attempts I gave him a little slap across his face. And I mean little. They didn't hurt him. They weren't supposed to. They were just to wind him up a bit more. Ha, ha. The look on his face.

Until then we were the only ones on either side of the road. But now there were a couple of cars approaching us from behind this dick's car. He knew he had to get moving so he started to wind his window back up. Just before it got to the end he looked me in the eye and spat in my face. I wasn't too angry because he had needed to come back at me with something. I couldn't have it all my own way. I did think about getting a hold of his tie before he wound up the window. Imagine that, me holding his tie outside while he's trying to drive off. It would've been like something from a cartoon. The engine revving and the wheels spinning and the car going nowhere.

He wound up the window completely and started to drive away. At this point a purely instinctive reaction overcame me. I swung my left leg in order to connect with the rear lights of the car as it passed me. I gave it a good whack and managed to smash the reverse light. I saw the plastic shade fall to the ground as the car drove away. Then I went into the park for my run.

On my way home I stopped off at the shop down the road. I was standing in front of the wine shelves contemplating which to buy when a man comes, stands in front of me and does exactly the same. Was my view so great that he had to steal it? I told him, 'Excuse me' and tapped him on his shoulder. He then complained about me touching him and that the shelves are for everybody. I said it was rude to block my view like he did. Then he made me laugh because he said something like, 'What are you gonna do about it?' and I said I'd already moved him out of the way. Then he said, 'What are you gonna do about it now?' and I took the hint, I knew what he meant. I wanted a bit of fun first though. I told him I don't hit men with glasses. So he took his off and started grinning. Then he told me that thing that man's greatest fear is telling someone 'I don't hit men with glasses' in order to avoid fighting then upon seeing the man take them off you realise you have to fight. 'That's how the story goes' I told him before smashing a bottle of red over his head.

And then just as I was approaching the front door to my flat I had a little flare up with this old man who, I don't know, might have been somebody when he was young and probably thought he still was. He wasn't old old but was older than I think he thought he was. He was wearing an all white suit and a white sun hat. He looked like a cricket umpire. He was rushing up the pavement towards me and there was a woman who was walking ahead of me and on the same side as him so, you know, the two of them were on a collision course. She stepped over to her left to avoid him but he went that direction too. He was in a greater hurry than her and was walking quicker than her so it was harder for him to swerve away from her and change direction. I understood that. But I didn't understand why he had to slag her off. He said something like 'Get out of the damn way you fool!' I know, it sounds like Mr T was having a go. If Mr T ate cucumber sandwiches. And he said it loud too. He didn't mutter it or say it under his breath. At first I just thought he was a grouchy old man having a bad day. But then as he passed me he said something about her being a stupid woman with no respect.

So I stopped and quickly walked after him. I grabbed him by the arm and told him there was no need for that. Of course he said 'Get your hands off me' in a twang that I'd expected him to. And then he said something like, 'How dare you touch me like this.' I almost burst out laughing. I then expected him to say something like, 'This is obscene. Unhand me at once.' But he didn't.

I imagined he owned a manor or estate somewhere and therefore owned the help who maintained it. This wasn't his manor though and here he didn't own anybody. I told him he couldn't go around talking to people like that and that he should find some manners from somewhere. Then he started to panic and say things like, 'What are you going to do to me?' I wasn't going to do anything; I was too tired after my run to do any more physical exercise or anything like that. I didn't tell him that though. I took a firmer grip on his arm and told him he was to go back to that woman and apologise. And that I would stand there and watch him. Also that from this day on he was to be on his best behaviour and treat everyone like the gentleman he was supposed to be. He nodded his head in agreement at our deal. He nodded a lot. Then I told him I knew where he lived and that I would check in on him now and then. He nodded his head a little more.

I moved my head in the direction of the woman as a signal that it was time to apologise and he duly started to walk after her. He turned back after a few metres to check I was still looking. And I was. I put two fingers to my eyes and then at him.
But that was that and I went inside. I couldn't be bothered to do any more.

Later it came to me that I should have asked for money not to beat him up. I could've made a nice little earner there. A nice little bunce.

Anyway, that was then and this is now. Like I say, this is my relaxing time. There's not going to be any trouble tonight. It's not the most comfortable I've ever been when watching football in a pub. Not a minute goes by with out me being nudged or my foot getting stepped on. I'm not angry though. Sometimes these things happen and this is one of those times. It's not only happening to me. But it really surprises me when I get shoved from behind and told, "Move somewhere else. You've been in the way ever since you arrived." I turn around to see some lad in a suit. He's studying the telly screen, probably needs to so he'll have an idea of what's going on. I bet he's only watching so he won't feel left out when everyone else is talking about it tomorrow. Now he looks at me. He gives me a look that says, 'You still here?' I ignore him. I want to see the game through to the end, there's not long to go now. I look at the people around us. A few of them heard what he said. No one else said anything though. I don't know if they agreed or disagreed.

The game's ended and most people are leaving the pub. It's almost like leaving the actual stadium, what with the amount of people and the wait to get through the exit. I finally get out and see everyone else disappear in each and every direction. I fancy a cigarette. I pull one out of my pocket but realise I don't have a lighter. Michaela must've taken it with her. I wouldn't normally mind as I don't often smoke, just now and then. And now. Partly because there's a girl smoking over there by the kerb. Asking to borrow her lighter could be a nice little icebreaker. And then Michaela can keep mine.

She's not bad. Let's see how this goes. If she's not up for it then it won't be a great loss.

"Could I borrow your lighter? I lost mine."

She doesn't say anything, just stares at me when she gives me it. She's got very blue eyes.

"Thanks, I was gagging for a fag." She continues staring, "I was going to say 'You saved my life'."

"Heh, heh." she lets out a giggle and shows me the sweetest smile

"Come on baby, let's go." says a voice. Then in front of me I see a man come into view and put his right arm around this girl. Then he takes a look at me, the intruder in his castle trying to serenade his queen. I wonder if he's going to piss around her next.

"It's you again." he says, his eyes lighting up, then smirking, "You're still in the way."

"You're the only one complaining sunshine. Maybe you're in the way. Maybe you should spend some time alone where no one's in the way."

The smirk's disappeared from his face. He takes his arm back from around the girl and steps towards me.

"You wanna fuck my girl?" he puts his face so close to mine I feel his stubble. "Is that what you want?

You wanna fuck my girl?" then he pokes me in the chest. "Fuck off. Or I'll kick the shit out of you."

"Yeah?"

He's got a real serious face on him now. He's staring at me without blinking and breathing very calmly. I wasn't much in the mood for a fight earlier but now after everything this boy's done tonight I'm coming around to the idea. On another night I would've ripped his head off for pushing me in the pub. This isn't another night though. I can't seem to get angry enough.

I'm sick of having his face so close to me though and I push him away from me. Then he surprises me with a punch to my mouth. For about a second I don't think about anything. Only the surprise has registered. I feel a couple more punches, hitting me on the ear and top of my head. Now I can taste blood in my mouth. I'm bleeding. This fucker's hurt me. He's shown me no manners tonight and now he's bloody cut my mouth.

I like the taste though. It makes me feel alive. It makes me feel that the fight will be worth it, and that the success will be sweeter.

He grabs my head with his left hand, steadying me so he can hit me with a cleaner punch. I beat him to it though. I give him two big punches to his ribs on his left side and he lets go of my head. It feels like I would have smashed them if I'd kept punching them. They felt hard and the impact hurt my hand but, like the blood in my mouth, the pain is spurring me on. It's like using your fist to knock down a wall instead of a mallet. You know you're doing it for a reason, there's a goal. And when you see the signs of the wall breaking you begin to taste the impending success. No pain can stop me. I could keep punching his ribs all day.

I've hurt him, I can see that. He steps about two feet away from me. I'm not going to let him escape. He wanted this fight and I'm not ready to finish it yet. I take a step towards him and swing my right fist into his cheek. He drops like a bag of potatoes. He won't be getting up for a while. I nearly drop as well. I didn't hold back on that one.

I stand over him, the fight won. I'm not finished though. I want to leave him with a memento. Something for both of us to remember this night by. Like the picture of Adam heaped on the ground that I have in my memory. I don't want another picture like that though. I want something else. Something special. Maybe I should crack his head open on the pavement. Or put him through a car window.

Something starts to break my concentration. During these fights I can't hear anything around me. I can only hear the fire burning between my ears, the emotion blowing through my body like a hurricane. The sound feels like being underwater. I suppose that's what rage sounds like. But now I can hear the sounds around me again. The traffic, dogs barking, a few murmurs behind me. I also hear this lad's girlfriend sobbing. I turn to her and see her standing over him just like me. Tears are flowing from her sweet blue eyes. Her face has turned a rosy pink. Her hands are clasped together in front of her mouth. I kneel down beside her boyfriend's head.

"No, no!" she cries in that broken voice women have when they're crying and rushes down to the other side of his head. "He's had enough. No more."

Her eyes widen and I stare into them. I can now see the redness in them brought by her crying. She looks beautiful. She's uncontrollably upset and she looks beautiful. I keep staring at her. She's hypnotised me. How can I hurt her any further? She's gone through enough. He deserves everything, but her? No.

"Please..?" she pleads one last time

But does she deserve him?

"Hey, he started all this. I didn't do anything. He started pushing me in the pub for no reason." I tell her calmly, hoping she understands. "And then he started the fight. It's not my fault he lost."

She closes her eyes and cries some more. I understand she's upset because of the state of her boyfriend but she surely understands that's the truth, no?

"Leave him now mate. Don't hurt him any more, eh?" says a voice behind me. I turn around and see a crowd gathered to see what the commotion's about. I don't know who it was who said that, it could've been anyone. Everyone's got the same pained expression on their faces. I turn back to my opponent/victim, whatever he is. He's coming around now, waking up. He looks like he just realised he has a headache. He probably needs someone to take a look at him.

I hear a siren somewhere. It sounds like police. Don't ask me why or how but I just know. It gets louder, like it's getting closer. I climb up from the ground and step over the body in front of me. I touch the girl's shoulder before walking away.

Chapter Fourteen

And this is where you find me, staring at the ceiling, up to date again. Now you might have some idea why I feel so strange. How did things get like this? I didn't sleep much last night. This night. The night just gone. It's morning now and I've barely slept. First I stayed up for a few hours with my hand covered in a frozen packet of peas. Then I lay in bed seeing the faces of that girl and those people behind us. I couldn't get them out of my head. Again and again I kept seeing them. Why? What does it mean?

I stare up at the white ceiling. I think it's going to be one of those days. Staring at a white ceiling, a blank white canvas. Maybe I'll switch to looking out of the window later. In any case I don't feel up to much. I feel tired and exhausted. Overworked and stressed out. This could well be a day I imagine I'm someone else with someone else's problems. I have enough of my own. I don't even have enough energy to get up and make a coffee. I almost feel strapped to the bed. I suppose missing one coffee won't be so bad – it will help me have a nap later. Or now. I don't even know if

I'm awake. My eyes keep flickering. I'm dozing in and out of a slumber.

The white ceiling's getting darker, greyer in fact. Someone's here with me, someone's approaching me. I turn quickly and sharply to my right. That hurt. It feels like whiplash in my neck and brain freeze in my head.

I see Michaela standing over me, checking I'm awake. She looks emotionless. Not happy, nor sad. And definitely not apologetic. Maybe she was stealing things before I woke up. I turn back away from her. My neck hurts in that position.

"Are you ok? Are you awake?"

"Aha" she can't rob me now

"How are you feeling? Do you want me to get you anything?"

I shake my head and look back at the ceiling. It interests me more at the moment.

"I was worried about you."

So worried I haven't seen or heard from her for weeks.

She sits down beside my bed, shifting her gaze between me and the floor. She doesn't seem too comfortable to be here. I don't suppose she would. She should feel guilty for being away so long.

"I've been staying at my friend Rebecca's. I needed some time on my own. I thought about you though. I wanted to get in touch but wasn't sure if you wanted me to. You never got in touch with me…"

It's good to hear her. I'm still staring at the ceiling but I'm listening to everything she's saying. But I don't want to show her too much attention.

She stops talking and sits in silence for a few minutes. I hear her fidgeting in her seat and looking around. I finally turn to her. She sees me looking at her and turns back to me. We stare at each other, neither saying a word. I have a thousand things I'd like to say but can't think of a single one right now. She senses that I want to say something.

"Say something, please. Anything. Just say…"

"Why did you go away?"

"I told you I needed to get away, to get some time on my own."

"But why? What was wrong?"

She seems uncomfortable talking about it. She looks away from me, at the bed, around the room, out of the window. I feel like I have the upper hand. I should be able to press a better explanation out of her.

"I just felt confused. I saw a side of you I hadn't seen before and wasn't sure if it was one I wanted to see."

"Maybe it was always there and you hadn't wanted to see it."

"Maybe. But that doesn't mean I have to like it, does it?"

"No." She's right about that I'll admit. But why did she have to run off like that and not get in touch? Couldn't she at least tolerate it? I have so many questions, I'm going to forget half of the ones I want to ask.

"What didn't you like about it?"

"It felt like you wouldn't be there to protect me. A woman needs to feel that her man will always be there to defend and protect her. I didn't feel that from you. You wanted to talk and negotiate instead of fighting."

Should I tell her about the fighting I've done while she's been gone? Will that make her feel better?

"And for what? For some idea that you could help society? That you could show people the errors of their ways?"

She looks at me like I'm talking about aliens.

"Yeah. This is what every good-living person wants but doesn't do anything about. It has to start somewhere, why not with me?" In my head it sounds like the most natural thing in the world.

"It sounds like a great idea, it does, but why would anyone listen to you sweetie?" Sweetie really cushioned the blow. "Would a bank robber or murderer really stop and listen to you? Do you really believe that?"

"Those are two bad examples. They would come later on. First I would have to work on muggers, like the guy who stopped us, and rude and impolite people."

"Ok fair enough, I understand. It's a good idea but why should you do it? This kind of thing would need a celebrity to promote it, for PR. Someone like Bono or him from Coldplay. People are more likely to listen to them than you."

That's possibly the most painful thing anyone's said to me.

"And what do you mean by rude and impolite people? You can't change them."

Again, she says it like it's impossible.

"Why not?" A simple question I believe. "If someone's rude or impolite they should be told about it. Then hopefully they'll behave better in future."

"But…" she's struggling for words. She knows she's wrong. "But you can't change people's behaviour or mannerisms to suit you. What's to say that you're not rude or impolite? You're not perfect, you know?"

I stare at the ceiling again. It understands me and doesn't talk back to me.

"I'm sorry for being ideological. I'm sorry for trying to change something instead of just moaning about it to anyone who'll listen."

She looks down at the ground, not looking so happy with what I said. She understands that was a thinly veiled attack on her. When with friends, at work, or on her Facebook page she always complains of people doing this and that. But she never tries to do anything about it. 'It's society's problem.' she always says.

And who is society?

I lay and she sits in silence for a few minutes. It's fine with me. The silence feels precious. If we speak anymore I feel the prickliness will continue and she'll end up leaving. It hasn't been a great welcoming for her. I haven't laid out the welcome mat. I haven't even got out of bed. I don't know what she expected though. I haven't heard from her for weeks, why's she here now?

I'm glad she's here though. I don't want her to leave yet. It feels like I needed someone to talk to. Someone to share things with.

"How has it gone? Have you had any altercations with muggers or rude people?" she asks tentatively, looking at the lines on her hands

"This is London, what do you think?" she smiles "A few things have happened. I've tried to put my ideas into action a few times."

"And?" she keeps looking at her hands, apparently not interested in what I have to say. She might as well be asking me about the weather or what I had for dinner last night

"In truth, sometimes I've had to fight fire with fire."

"What do you mean?"

"Sometimes people have been violent or aggressive towards me and I've needed to do likewise."

"Ok. In what way?"

"Well. Some people weren't so willing to listen to what I was saying and started trouble."

"What kind of trouble?"

"They'd get aggressive and want to fight."

"Yeah...?" she says in a disbelieving tone "And you fought fire with fire, did you?"

"Yeah."

She stares at me, at my eyes, waiting expectantly for me to crack. Like a witness with an unconvincing story under interrogation from the police.

"And how did that go?"

"Alright. Some times were better than others. Shame you weren't around to see for yourself."

Pow! Take that!

"You don't have any marks on your face, you must've done ok."

Is she being serious?

"My hand's hurt if you want proof. I had ice on it last night."

She nods, unconvincingly.

"What happened last night?"

"I had a fight with someone in a pub. I was watching football on the telly, it was busy and someone started pushing me because I was standing too close to him."

"Aha. So you had a fight with him?"

"Yeah. I didn't want to but he attacked me."

"But tell me, did you get beaten up or did you have a fight?"

"What do you mean?"

"You say he was pushing you and then attacked you. Did you do anything to him?"

"Yeah, I smashed his ribs and almost knocked him out."

"You did?"

"Yeah. His girlfriend begged me to stop hitting him. Otherwise I…"

"Otherwise you might've done even more damage."

She definitely said that tongue-in-cheek.

"Don't you believe me or something? My hand is really bad. I had it in ice for hours last night before going to bed."

She can't take her eyes off my hand now. She looks to be studying it for damage.

"I can't see any bruises or cuts. Maybe it's all inside. Maybe it's broken."

She doesn't believe it's broken, she says it too mockingly. Like when you lose something as a child and your mum says it was fairies who took it.

"You don't believe me, do you?"

"Why do you say that?" she sniggers. She actually means, 'Why would I believe you?'

"You just don't look like you do." I tell her "You're not sympathetic for my hand and you find it hard to believe that I could do such things."

"Well, I only need to think back to the last time I saw you. You said you wanted to straighten out criminals without getting your hands dirty. Now you're telling me you're knocking out men who push you in a pub. And I can think about everything I've known about you through the years."

"Next time I'll cut his head off and hang it on the wall for you as proof. How about that?"

"It just doesn't seem like you or something you'd do."

"Well you've been away a while, some things have changed. You should stick around this time; you might like what you'll see."

She smirks at that remark. I don't think she believes that either.

"I wish everything could be solved without violence or aggression, that's my ultimate aim, but some wars are just necessary. I'm not going to let someone beat me without giving some back. I'll probably always be prepared for violence. Look at Switzerland, they have an army. Maybe one day they'll need it. And their knives."

She looks a little more convinced now. Or tired from protesting. I get the impression though that she's withholding something from me, that there's something on the tip of her tongue.

"But it's not going smoothly, is it?" she says this in a quiet serious voice. I don't understand why she thinks this.

"It's going ok. I've told you that."

"But it's not though, is it?" Why does she say that? Can she see a bruise on my face or something? "It's not going ok because otherwise you wouldn't be in this situation, would you?"

In what situation? What does she mean?

I see a tear drop from her left eye. Why is she crying?

"Why have you done this to yourself? How have you gone from that to this?"

"Things just happened. I don't really want to fight with people but sometimes it just happens."

"I don't mean that!" she interrupts sternly, though her voice is breaking. "Stop it. Stop talking about what you've wanted and not wanted to do and instead tell me about why you're here now."

She looks away from me out of the window. I see the sunlight shine on the tear marks on her cheeks and the tear gloss in her eyes. Her face begins to crease again and more tears flow. She puts her hands to her face.

"Why did you try to kill yourself?"

Is she crazy? Me? I didn't try to kill myself. Maybe she has me confused with another boyfriend.

"What? I didn't try to kill myself."

She manages to stop herself from crying and wipes away the tears from her cheeks.

"You didn't? Then why are you lying in a hospital bed connected to all these machines?"

"What are you talking about? We're at home, this is our bed."

She moves her chair around next to my head so she can get the same view as me. She looks out across the room.

"Look around you. This isn't home."

I look around and see many more beds. I see different types of people in the beds, young and old, black and white. Some look better than others. Some have people sitting outside the beds, some don't. Those who do don't seem to be talking. I can see lips moving and heads nodding and shaking but there's no sound. The only sound I hear is the silence. The room is so silent and that silence is loud. It's deafening.

And everything's white. The bed sheets, the gowns, the walls, the floor. The ceiling too I notice. It looks just like mine at home. I can't tell the difference.

I look down at what's immediately in front of me. I see a white duvet on a big single bed. There's some kind of railing at the foot of the bed. I look at my arm. I see a tube poking into my wrist with some tape holding it in place. I wonder where the tube is from. I follow it with my eyes until it goes past my head between me and where Michaela is sitting. I turn my neck and see the tube is connected at the other end to a big plastic bag full of a weird-looking liquid. I don't know if it's going in or out of my wrist. Again my neck hurts in this position so I turn back to look ahead.

I don't feel like I'm part of this room. I feel like I'm just sitting here watching it. It has nothing to do with me. No one is looking at me like I am at them or wondering what's wrong with me. They can't see me. When the doctors come they won't speak to me. There'll be nothing to say. There's nothing wrong with me.

I glance over towards Michaela. She seems to be looking around the room in the same way as I am. Is she even here? Is this all a dream?

"Is this real?" I ask her.

She turns to me and nods, reluctantly it looks like.

"What happened? Why am I here?"

"That's what I've been asking you about."

I don't understand this. And I don't like it. I want to go home. Everything's too loud here. And too white. Too loud and too white.

"How long have I been here?"

"More than a week, the doctor says."

More than a week. And I didn't even know. More than a week in this bed. In this room with these people. How couldn't I know that?

"Why am I here?"

"You took a load of pills which rendered you unconscious. You were found in the nick of time and the doctors were able to save you."

"Save me? From what?"

"From death." she says, staring at me through my eyes. "You took enough pills to take your life."

But when was this? I only took those pills I got from that man to build up my muscles. He didn't say anything about them killing me.

"When was this? It wasn't me. Someone must've put the pills in my mouth while I was sleeping."

Michaela shakes her head in denial. She's right, that does sound ridiculous, but what else could it be?

"They're treating it as a suicide attempt."

She stares at me for a reaction. I don't have one. Except for a confused expression.

"Suicide? No… I didn't attempt suicide."

"What then?" she really wants an explanation. She demands an answer.

I don't have one.

"I don't know."

Chapter Fifteen

I feel myself waking up. I'm trying to refuse by keeping my eyes shut. It's been a nice sleep. Very deep and peaceful. I've no idea for how long. It's still daytime but I don't know if it's the same day. In fact I don't know what day it is. Everything's confusing me just now.

It feels that this is it now, I'm awake. There's no going back to hiding in my sleep. It's time to deal with whatever's out there.

I open my eyes and see a white ceiling again. The same one that looks like the one in the hospital and also in my home. Which one is this?

I look over and see a man in a bed opposite with heavily bandaged wrists and forearms. I can see small patches or big dots of blood seeping through them. I wonder how he feels. Is he sad he's still alive? Or happy he's got another stab at life? What has this experience taught him?

What has this experience taught me? I don't have a clue. I'm still not sure what this experience is.

I don't see Michaela anywhere. Where is she? Maybe she's run away again. Was she even here at all? I don't know what's real at the moment.

"Hello." a voice comes from my right and I see someone approach the bed. It's Michaela. "I was waiting for you to wake up."

"Aha…" I'm still not sure this is real.

"How did you sleep?"

"Ok. I wasn't sure where I was going to wake up,"

"Your mum and dad were here. They were sad you weren't awake to speak to them."

Sorry, my sleeping patterns are a little off at the moment.

"They've gone home for a little rest themselves. They'll be back later. Your mum brought some photos to put beside your bed. She read somewhere they'll help you become more positive, and even retain that spirit during your sleep."

She places out some photos on the bed cover in front of me. They're all from my trip to South America two years ago. I see the bright colours and bustle of Buenos Aires, the blue Atlantic Ocean on the Argentinian coast, the enormous sand dunes on the Chilean side. I see mountain tops, volcano peaks and accessible hillsides that I was too afraid to scale.

I know the reason for this is well-intended, but I can't help feeling worse. These are pictures of a happy time on the other side of the world, far away from where I am now emotionally and physically. The fact I'm here rather than there saddens me. Sure I could go back there to recuperate once I'm out of here but that'd cost money I don't have. Plus what's to say my problems wouldn't still be waiting for me afterwards.

"The doctor was here too. He'll be back later; he thought it best not to wake you."

"Hmm, ok."

"He told me a few things."

"Ok." I don't have anything else to say. She's the one with all the answers. I wonder what he said.

"He said you were brought in here with a cocktail of pills inside you. They pumped your stomach but something happened and you slipped into unconsciousness until yesterday."

It's like being told about your life after losing your memory. Or being told about everything you did whilst being drunk at the party the night before.

"They're not completely happy with your condition so they're going to keep you here under their supervision. They want to be sure you don't have a bad reaction to their treatment."

That's fine. I don't feel like going home right now. And at least here I get free room and board.

"Do you remember any of this?"

"Not really, no." I shake my head.

She looks bemused, like she neither knows what to say or do. How does she think I feel?

"I got hold of some pills from someone. He said they would make my muscles bigger and stronger. I didn't think this would happen though."

"They weren't steroids that you took, they were something else. And you took too many. That's why this happened."

She looks at me like a parent does when they want the truth from their child by pretending to be their best friend. What makes her think I know so much about what happened? I didn't even realise I was in hospital.

"Why did you take so many pills?"

"I thought that by taking more the process would work more quickly. Obviously I was wrong."

She nods in agreement.

"But," I knew there was something else she wanted to say. She looks away from me as she says it though. "you didn't want to kill yourself?"

"No. Why would I want to do that?"

"I don't know." she turns back to me, "You've been behaving strangely lately. I'd never had thought that you would want any such drugs until now. And for what? To defend yourself?"

Great, we're back to this again.

"And then there are some of the things you've been talking about."

"What things?" What things does she mean?

"About knocking people out outside pubs for example, that's not you. That's not who I fell in love with."

"Maybe that's not who you knew. You didn't like me, remember, so you went away and I was left alone. Was I supposed to just wait for you to come back?"

It looks like the waterworks are going to start again. That's not what I want but I'm not just going to lie here and have her say all this to me.

"Look," I lower my voice and try to sound more diplomatic for the conversation was getting heated there and people were looking over. "the last time I saw you, you said some damaging things. Things that made me

100

look at myself and things I didn't like. I tried to do something about it and, now it doesn't appear to have gone too well, but for a while I felt exhilarated and alive. I regret a little of what happened the other night but the nights that preceded it I don't regret at all. Now if that was down to the pills, then…"

"What about the other night?" she interrupts, lifting her gaze from the floor

"The night outside the pub. I had a fight with this lad. I told you…"

"That didn't happen." she interrupts again. Her tears have stopped and she appears more serious-looking now. "Don't you see?"

See what? She moves herself closer towards me.

"You say that happened the other night, but you were here. Don't you realise that? For the last week or so you've been here in this bed."

She's definitely spelling it out for me. She's beating me with these words, these revelations.

"That night at the pub didn't happen." And there's the final blow.

But it must've happened. It seems so clear. I remember all the details.

"What about my hand? My hand hurt like hell afterwards."

She shakes her head.

"I asked the doctor to take a look at it while you were sleeping. He says it's fine, normal. It doesn't even need an x-ray. He says you haven't punched anyone with it."

How can this be?

Chapter Sixteen

I sit on my knees surrounded by bodies. Laid out in front of me is the body of the man I've just put there. His face is pale and looks disjointed due to the heavy punches I've given it. His eyes are closed and he's not moving, but he's not dead. Opposite me is his girlfriend crouching at the side of his head. I remember her crying the last time I saw her but now she just looks at me disappointingly, like I'm stupid. I don't know why. I remember the sorrow of the previous time I was here. I felt bad for bringing pain and sadness to her.

I look up and see a man standing over me. His clothes have stained patches all over them. I don't know what that's from. I look at his face and see a large gash on the side of his forehead. Blood is pouring from it and running down the side of his face. His face is wet and pink with something else though, red wine it looks like. The claret and crimson are forming a new shade on his left cheek. I've seen this shade before. A few weeks ago in the supermarket, this same man was lying face down in a puddle of it on the ground. I remember the exhilaration of seeing him there, the thrill of me putting him there.

Now I see the whiteness of the hospital room. The very bright whiteness. The sun is shining through the windows and everything is bathed in its light. I must have fallen back to sleep. I feel a cold sweat around my neck and my patient gown's sticking to me. I must have had a nightmare.

"Hello." says a voice on my right. I turn and see a long white coat with two biro pens poking out of the outside breast pocket. One blue, one black. The coat is buttoned up but at various gaps I can see there's a green shirt underneath it. I look up and see the face of the man wearing the white coat. Most of his face is hidden by a pair of those thick-rimmed NHS glasses you used to get. I suspect he got his from somewhere else. I can see the designer's name on the side frame but I can't be bothered to read it. I look down again and see a clipboard in his hands. Everything together leads me to believe he's my doctor. Oh, and there's a stethoscope around his neck.

"I thought it might be you. I wanted to see you first to make sure. You went to All Saints', didn't you?"

"The primary school?" He nods several times in quick succession. "Yes, I did."

"It's me, Adam Nielsen. Remember? We had Mr James and Mrs Hamlett as teachers. I don't remember the others' names."

"Oh.." There we go, I guess I didn't leave him in a bloody mess in the park a few weeks back. Hooray for that.

"When I saw your name I wondered if it was you. Then I saw your next of kin, I remember your mum, I thought it must be."

Yep, it's me. I can only smile.

"And you're a doctor now?"

"Yeah." he's happy to say, looking at his white coat. "I've been here for about two years."

The pride and self-love in his face make me think it's a prestigious hospital to work in. I'm not paying to stay here, am I?

"Anyway, enough about all that for now. I am your assigned doctor. While you're here you're in my care. Now, tell me, how are you feeling?"

"Not too bad." the truth.

He looks at his clipboard.

"I believe your partner Michaela has given you the gist of your condition." Yeah, nurse Michaela did. "Don't worry, I'm not going to bore you with the details just yet."

Thank science for that.

I stare into an empty space and concentrate on nothing while he continues speaking. I can only hear a muffled noise affecting my daydreaming. He's probably saying something important; he's a doctor after all. I should zoom back in.

"I must stress to you that while we're pleased with your progress so far, you're not out of the woods yet. You'll be staying with us for the foreseeable future."

What does that mean, 'foreseeable future'? I can foresee today, tomorrow and next year. Which is it? For now though I just nod, I'm not in the mood for a big discussion over my well-being. I just want to be.

"Also, at some point we're going to let a therapist speak to you, to root out what happened and why, to make sure it doesn't happen again." His face becomes serious-looking as it leans into mine, "Nothing is worth killing yourself for. There's always hope. Remember me at school, how I used to behave? What an idiot, eh? But look, I got my act together and came out the other side. You can too."

And he points his finger at me three times to reinforce the last bit, 'you can too'. At least he didn't make us high five each other. He takes his face back to a suitable distance from mine. It lights up knowing he's satisfied another customer. I expect him to pull out a lollipop for me, but no. Instead he turns and walks away towards another unsuspecting invalid.

'Remember me at school, how I used to behave?' Is he kidding? I remember pummelling his

105

face at the park. Or at least I remember the dream or whatever that now was. He was a fool back in school though. It didn't bother me much back then as it was his problem. I always tried to ignore him and his tantrums. But then I felt so much satisfaction in beating him up. Why? Why did it suddenly bother me enough to hurt him? And in my subconscious even.

At least I'll have something to talk to the therapist about.

Chapter Seventeen

I lay now in a different bed in a different room. This could probably be the finest room in the hospital. It has colour, furniture and ornaments. And it smells normal. I get the impression it's been designed to suit someone's taste rather than be neutral so as to not offend or displease any sick patients. The walls are painted dark blue. Not navy, a little lighter. On the wall in front of me I can see a black picture frame containing a white and grey photo of a flower. Next to that I see a large bookcase. In any other room this bookcase would be the dominant feature but here its varnished wood and many books of different sizes are toned down by the room's colour scheme.

I move my head slightly to the right and see a long window half obscured by brown wooden blinds. Between two of the blinds I can see something flying, a wasp or a fly. I can vaguely hear the blinds knocking each other as it crashes into them. Below the window is a wide white window sill adorned with various plants, a vase of flowers and something in a frame that looks like a degree.

Sitting by the window behind the desk is my host. She's in one of those nice big reclining chairs that all office managers have. All the good ones anyway. She's dressed in a black trouser suit and looks very elegant in a minimalist way, or whatever they call it. Her hair's tied up at the back of her head by what looks like a pencil or a black chopstick. She's pretty, I can't escape that view. I wish we could've met in different circumstances, with her not seeing me in this state. She sits crossed legged with a notepad resting on her left knee. She told me I can start whenever I feel ready. Today it'll just be me talking and her listening. She said I can talk about anything I want. I glance over to my left now and see a long black leather couch beside the wall next to the door. I suppose that's where the patients usually sit and talk. For me today though I'm on a hospital trolley. They thought it'd be easier this way with all my wires and tubes and things. Getting onto that couch will be my aim for the time being.

I look up at the ceiling and sigh.

"I don't really know what I'm doing here to be honest. Until a few days ago I didn't even know I was here. It seems I swallowed too many pills and was brought here to be saved, to be saved from dying. But you know that already. I didn't mean for it to happen. That's the truth. I didn't know this would happen, otherwise I wouldn't have done it."

107

"I took the pills because I was sick of being pushed around by people. I thought the pills would make me stronger, give me a better physique and I'd have a fairer chance of winning fights. Though don't get me wrong, I don't go looking for fights with people, the opposite's closer to the truth. But you know sometimes things happen, emotions run high and suddenly fists are flying. I just wanted to be a bit better prepared that's all."

"Also, guys with muscles are shown more respect, they're even feared sometimes, you know? People rarely start trouble with them or show them disrespect. No one ever listens to me. I'm just there in the background, what I think doesn't matter, I'm expected to do what anyone says."

"You know I had a big plan a while back. Something that would get me noticed, something people would admire. I wanted to advise and influence everyone to be nice to each other and show each other respect. I hate when people get angry because someone's looking at them. What's the problem? Of all the bad things that can happen, why get angry over that? It doesn't matter. Concentrate on the important things like loving your family and friends. Smile, laugh, be happy, respect one another. Then I thought about criminals, you know, thieves and thugs. Why do they do this? Why can't someone reason with them, explain it's not right? Instead of dismissing them as an underclass and blaming society, why not do something about it ourselves? For a start we could find out why they're doing it, stealing for example. Maybe they're unemployed, unlikely to get a job due to a lack of education. Maybe they were abandoned or badly treated by their parents, who knows? I don't think society, as we call ourselves, can just throw these people into the rubbish bin. Like, 'it didn't work with these, let's forget about them'. Let's help them get a job somewhere, help them cope with their childhood. Give food and shelter to those who need it. If they were jumping off a bridge you'd help them, why not now? They're still throwing their lives away."

"A lot of those people have had problems growing up or maybe just bad luck but they deserve a second chance. If the people who want to see them disappear were in the same position, they would want a second chance."

"Do you know that I went to school with Dr Nielsen? I didn't know him too well, nor see him that much, but what I did see of him, I didn't like. He'd always get so angry at the smallest thing and would shout and scream at you right in front of your face. It was like a dog barking at an intruder. Goodness knows why he did that. I don't know what was going on with him then, what problems he had. But look at him now, a doctor. I didn't think for a second that he'd leave our school and become a doctor. Maybe you're going to tell me that he still barks like a rottweiler. In any case he's done well for himself and I take my hat off to him. There's hope for everyone."

"There's even hope for me. I talk and think about helping others but what am I doing myself? What great example am I showing? I'm almost 30 years old and working at the bottom of the ladder in a restaurant. My ambitions are nowhere near being realised anytime soon. My girlfriend thinks I'm a wimp and doesn't respect me. Sometimes I am a complete prat and I cringe at things I've said and done. I got beaten up by a policeman for behaving like a prat. The happiest I've felt in ages was when I was beating people up in, what I've since found out, were dreams. Typical. The best parts of my life are imaginary and fantasy. There I'm a different person, a better person. I'm nothing in reality. If I die today my life will have been a waste."

I look to my right and see my host scribbling away at her pad. She stops and looks up at me, smiling sympathetically. "Ok? All done?"

"For now."

'If I die today my life will have been a waste.' It goes round and round my head. I can't escape it. It's on a tape loop inside my head. It's true though, there's no avoiding that fact. They say that the biggest problem for addicts is admitting they have a problem. I'm not an addict but I do have a problem, and I admit it.

The question now is what do I do about it?

I should embrace this challenge and opportunity. I remember years ago thinking that I would voluntarily enter myself into a mental hospital so that I could use the time away from work to get my life's plans in order. Or I would become a priest, in which case I'd get free housing and not much work to do. I've kind of reached that goal now, except for the volunteering bit and the part with the doctors poking and pulling me. Oh, and me almost dying. Aside from that, if you think about it I've got some time on my hands now to sort out what I want to do with my life, so it's not a waste. Where do I start? Things to do, experiences to experience.

Chapter Eighteen

The room looks different this time, the walls are darker and there are more shadows. The light's artificial. A lamp on her desk is on and the window blinds are drawn. This time I notice that the picture of the flower on the wall is a drawing. It's good. My host isn't sitting behind her desk this time, in fact I can't see where she is. I can only hear her voice.

"It's good that you're able to observe your world around you. I believe you realise the proximity of death, that it's near. It could be today, tomorrow or in 30 years but it's near. It hovers over you, me and everybody. It's important you fulfil your life during this time. Be happy, be content. I'm intrigued that you want to help others, people who are strangers. This is something you should continue. I think you've only scratched the surface so far, your work is far from over. When the occasion presents itself, you'll know what to do. This will be your legacy, how you'll be perceived by others."

I can feel someone or something touching me. It's stroking my hair. Now the side of my face. My eyes open and I'm faced against the wall. The person touching me is on the other side, out of sight. It's a shame, now I can't pretend to be asleep and peek through my eyes. I'll have to wake up and turn over.

"Are you awake?"

I am now. I open my eyes fully and see Michaela sitting on the side of my bed.

"Yes." I say as I stifle a yawn.

"You were muttering in your sleep. What were you dreaming about?"

"I don't know. I didn't realise I was muttering. Maybe the dream will come back to me later."

"Yeah." She strokes my hair again, styling it into how she wants to see it. She's lucky I don't have a mirror handy. "How do you feel today?"

"Ok." A little tired, but there you go, I've just been woken up.

"Hopefully you'll be able to go home soon." she says like it's the news we're all waiting for, the thing that's going to make everyone happy. "See what the doctor thinks later."

"Yeah." I linger on that word 'hopefully'. I don't really hope to go home soon; I'd rather stay here a little longer. Here I'm looked after without any pressure to get on with things, nor any distractions. I feel I'm slowly using the time to sort some things out, to get some clarity.

112

She begins to follow the crease in the bed with her finger. She's probably thinking of something important and/or serious. I should probably brace myself. I see her mouth open, here it comes.

"Have you thought about what you'll do when you come out of here?"

"A little bit."

"And…?" her finger still tracing the lines in the cotton.

"You know it feels like I've been given a warning, that you don't know what's waiting for you around the corner. It also feels like I've been given a second chance."

She nods, though it doesn't look convincing, more like she's doing it in understanding of what I'm saying rather than agreeing.

"You have to make your life worthwhile, don't waste it. Don't have any regrets."

"Uh huh." she nods again. "Were you wasting your life before?"

I know where this is going.

"No." I shake my head. "No, I wasn't. But I wasn't focused on what I was doing or what I wanted to do."

"And now you are focused…" her voice fades a little, I feel there are tears waiting. "on what you're doing?"

"I'm getting there. Being in here, having nothing to do, gives you a lot of time to think."

"And have you thought about me? Am I a part of your second chance at life?"

She looks at me now, probably wanting to see every aspect of my expression.

"I don't know."

Chapter Nineteen

The room is dark. All the lights are out. On the wall to my left I can see a vague shadow of light from the streetlights outside. In the darkness of the room I can also see the blue and green lights of the machines at various points. The silence is still deafening in this place, even during the night. I can hear buzzing from the machines, sounds I have no idea of, one that I know is a lucky man snoring. I wonder if everyone else is awake. Or dead.

I can't sleep tonight. I've stayed in the same position since they turned the lights off. In fact since visiting hours finished and Michaela left. That might be the last time I ever see her. I'm treating it that way in any case. I don't know what will happen in the future but I'm prepared for that being the last time.

It didn't go great but it wasn't horrendous either. I tried to be as honest as possible and encouraged her to do the same. I didn't see the point in us hiding things during such an important discussion. I told her that maybe we should spend some time apart, see how we do without each other, see if we'll miss each other. That didn't go down too well at first but I think I convinced her of its merits in the end. Not without any tears or signs of anger from her though. She blamed me for everything it seemed. All her problems were my fault. Her dissatisfaction at work, her inability to stop smoking, her waistline, all down to me. I pointed out to her that she should take a look at her own role in those issues. And to stop blaming me of course. I think it goes without saying that I reminded her of leaving me first. I regret now that I didn't ask her why she came back.

Maybe it's because she needs a man, any man to be there by her side, regardless of who. If it wasn't me then it could quite easily be someone else. I didn't get an answer when I suggested this to her.

And she left. That was that. I feel a little sad, that a part of my life is over. But where one door closes, another opens, and now I feel like I have a blank canvas in front of me. Now I must choose what I'll paint. Whatever it is I won't regret doing it. From now on I'll have no regrets about what I do, everything will be done for a reason and a good intention.

My eyes are closing now. I think some strange thoughts in my slumber and I probably won't remember this in the morning.

Chapter Twenty

Today's the day. I'm on my way to the airport, I'm going far away. Over to South America, to Chile and Argentina to be exact. I can't afford it and I'm going to have little money left when I get back but what's money for if not to spend and enjoy yourself? I was saving this money for a rainy day and today it's raining. I need to get away. I need a holiday after this imposed stay I've had in hospital. I need some time and space to think things over, to evaluate who I am and who I want to be. I have to take control of my life, what I want to do with it, where do I want it to lead? There has to be more out there. There has to be more than this.

I'm going alone. I'd be too distracted if I went with anyone. I'd get caught up in the fun of being abroad, and the drinking and the laughing at the strange foreign things. This way I'll be able to concentrate better and that will be more beneficial in the long term. Listen to me, I sound like I'm in a seminar.

The traffic's bad today in London. There seems to be road closures and single lanes everywhere. I suppose it's good my Dad made us leave early. It's just that now there's more time and dead air to kill in the car. I'm not in a very talkative mood, I haven't been for a while. Especially when it involves discussing recent events with my parents. All our conversations are coming back to that. And even the ones that aren't, I know it's on their minds. I realise they mean well and they're probably scared, but I'm not a baby anymore. What's more, I can manage most day-to-day tasks myself without being told how. How to iron a shirt for example. Or how to pack a bag.

At least today there's somebody else with us, my newborn nephew Andrew. He's been brought along for the ride to see the aeroplanes. Should be fun, he's been sleeping the last 30 minutes and was screaming before we left. I doubt he'll see anything either way.

It's pissy weather I'm leaving behind in London. It's been raining all the morning and all you can see is the evidence of that in the dull grey sky and wet roads. One good thing to come from it is the beautiful autumn leaves of the trees, yellows, reds, chestnut browns, like they've been hand painted by one of the Impressionists. The wet grass too is looking greener than usual. This is a good picture to remember England by – it won't look this way when I get back. Then there'll be no leaves, the tree barks and branches will be black and dying and the grass a muddy brown.
It must be hard for pilots in this weather. I can see the rain now swaying from side to side to the beat of the wind's tune. I wonder if they get paid extra for flying in such bad conditions.

My mind's wandering in the strangest avenues and this car's going nowhere in this traffic. I just want to be there now, without the waiting and travelling.

Chapter Twenty One

I'm now a step closer, I've made it onto the plane. It's full, it's going to be a busy flight. Already before take off there are lots of people fidgeting and getting up. And I can hear two babies crying. Things could be worse though. Sitting in the departure lounge before boarding I saw a pilot passing through the opposite gate carrying two duty-free bottles of whisky. I couldn't see where that flight was heading but I wish good luck to those passengers anyway. The pilot had a red face and bald head underneath his cap. He looked like Nikita Khrushchev. Or a James Bond baddie.
I really shouldn't be so judgemental. Maybe he planned on sharing the booze around.

At least I'm sharing a row of seats with a nice-looking pretty girl. Hopefully she'll make these 14 hours more tolerable. I'll try to find out more about her during the flight. I'm not too sure how though to be honest. My confidence, especially with women, is at zero at the moment. Me and Michaela are finished. We'll see what happens in the future but that's the situation for now at least. I realise I need to get back on the horse or the saddle, or whatever the Chinese cookie advice is, but right now that target seems too high. Hopefully this trip will help me in that regard, that's part of the plan, but I'd prefer to be tested at a later date. Preferably when the plane's arrived. I'd do well to remember beggars can't be choosers. Though I wouldn't class myself a beggar yet.

But sometimes women, or opportunities with women, just fall into your lap without you even trying. Sometimes when a girl's drunk. Not taking advantage in an immoral and illegal way, but of the moment because she'll be sober in the morning and full of regret. When a girl's upset is a common one, for much the same reasons as above. Sometimes when I'm drunk and behaving in a manner the opposite to normal, i.e. interesting, confident and/or funny. Not having anywhere to stay or not wanting to get the night bus/last train home is another one, mainly due to convenience.

Or there's what happened to me.

The plane hadn't yet taken off and there were discussions about seat places and baggage space and lots of swapping about of people and baggage. The majority of the women sitting around me were of a past generation and had given up exercise a few generations before that. One in particular sat opposite the aisle from me had no role in the matter, yet was a keen observer. Over both shoulders she kept twisting her neck, almost 180 degrees each time, to get a better look at what was going on. Every now and then she seemed to mutter something, apparently to herself. I didn't manage to catch what she said. Probably something about what she would do if she was in charge. A handful of the women then stood up to play musical chairs. An aeroplane isn't an ideal place to play such games, and especially not the thin aisle between the seats. That way

119

someone's going to get hurt, or get two large bum cheeks in their face – which was what I got.

At least it was worth seeing the passenger on my other side smile and laugh at the sight.

Chapter Twenty Two

And now I've arrived in Argentina. Sitting in a cab on Monday morning in Buenos Aires. The traffic's bad, people don't seem to be in much of a hurry to get to work- it could be Monday morning anywhere. Actually I'm not sure what sets Buenos Aires apart from other cities. Its wide boulevards and Latin air could lead you to believe you were in any number of cities in Italy or Spain. And it's busy and hectic pace could make you think you were in just about any big city. Or maybe it's just me. Or maybe it's globalisation. Maybe everywhere's bleeding into one giant blob of the same. Or maybe it's just me.

Buenos Aires doesn't feel like London however. Maybe because London's my home and this isn't I can easily differentiate the two. Maybe it's England's conservatism and Argentina's lack of it.

I can't decide whether it's a good idea to begin this trip in the big city or if I should've come here later. Anyway it's done now and I'm here. Let's enjoy it.

I'm staying in the same hostel as I did two years ago. It made a big impression on me then so it seems natural to stay here again. They're very welcoming and laid-back here. And very friendly too. They remember your name quickly. The mood of the hostel is to resemble an art studio and there are several paintings around, for sale too, as well as different sculptures and works used as decoration or practical use. Windows made of glass bottles for example, altering the colour of the sunlight shining through. The hostel gives free tango classes a couple of nights a week, as well as 24 hour use of the kitchen to guests. All around me I feel the Latin mantra of 'mi casa es su casa'. And all of this for a very affordable price in an upcoming tourist area.

I remember thinking two years ago that I couldn't picture such a place in London and that maybe it was up to me to create it. Ok, the rent would be higher in London and for all the fine hospitality I'm not sure how well this hostel does financially. I don't know what happened to that idea. It disappeared somewhere down the cracks, out of sight and out of mind.

This reminds me of a conversation I had with a Spanish girl staying in the hostel at the same time two years ago. This was at the end of my 6 month stay in these same countries and as time had passed the news from home was getting worse and worse and seemingly more apocalyptic. It was the time of the global recession and credit crunch. Banks had been given millions of pounds to clean up their mess and from what I could gather from where I was, no one was happy. No one wanted this to happen again. People wanted things to change. I wondered if my impending return home was to be greeted with whispers of revolution.

This Spanish girl said things couldn't continue as they were, that governments couldn't take our money to help badly-run businesses, that nobody consulted the public on such matters and that the voting, tax-paying public was basically a powerless spectator to the farce being played out in front of us. A farce that was people's lives unfortunately. I don't believe she exactly breathed the word 'revolution', but she certainly said things had to change. People had to take responsibility for their actions and control of their possessions. Don't rely on banks to protect all of your money, don't let supermarkets control the price of fruit and vegetables, it's possible to grow your own. Don't let so much food be unnecessarily wasted.

We'd held the hands of our trusted guardians and were led down the wrong path. Now it was time to find our own way.

That morning chat over breakfast had got me feeling positive about the times ahead. That nothing would be impossible for anybody. Two years on and I don't feel as positive or as confident. I feel another part of me has been lost, eroded by the pollution of normality, conformity and routine. And fear too probably if I'm honest.

I maybe shouldn't have taken her words too much to heart. She also said she had a season ticket to Barcelona FC but didn't go to the recent Clásico game against Real Madrid because it was raining. I wonder what she's doing now, if she's doing any better than me.

Chapter Twenty Three

I'm not much of a person to visit every tourist attraction in the guide book. And if I do go, then I make up my own mind instead of letting them tell me what I'm supposed to be enjoying. One place I'm visiting in Buenos Aires is the Recoleta cemetery.

This is a cemetery in the city open to the public and the resting place to a few hundred people. There are no graves here, only tombs. Some are well-maintained and in fine condition, some are dirty with cobwebs setting up homes on them. Some have weeds growing around them, some are dusty and seem to be fading. Some are made of marble, some are made of concrete. They all have glass windows on them for people to look through.

I don't know whose job it is to take care of them, whether it's the local council, the caretaker of the cemetery or the relations of those dead. If it's the responsibility of the relations then I wonder why some look so well looked after and others not. Some sparkling with clean marble and polished windows and bright flowers outside. Others look ignored and in the state that that brings.

I see an inscription on a plaque outside one tomb that has the coffin of a dead soldier inside. It says simply, 'He lived his life to the full before it was taken away from him.' I suppose that's a good lesson to learn and remember. You never know when life's going to end so make use of it and enjoy it while you can.

I don't think I would come here often to see to someone's tomb. It's very public and having a peaceful solemn moment can be hard to come by I imagine. Plus there's its location. Surrounding the cemetery are many busy bars and restaurants frequented by those looking to enjoy themselves, not reflect on someone's passing. Immediately next door a large shopping centre is in the process of being built.

Around Buenos Aires I've seen graffiti in honour of the president's husband who died a few days before my arrival. He was the husband of the current president and was due to be a strong candidate in the next election. A fatal heart attack ended his wishes and plans and those of millions of Argentines. Now on walls around the city and on fences outside the parliament building I see messages of condolence to the Presidenta and the message that his spirit and his will live on. A cynic would point out that the handwriting looks very similar in all the messages, but I'm not going to pay attention to that. What does make me think is that to me, from an outside perspective, the Argentinian people, with or without the help of the media, seem to often pin all their hopes on one figure, whether it be the president, Peron, Maradona. There's always a battle to fight, a struggle to overcome, and someone needs to be the one to lead from the front. I wonder how that feels. I can't imagine anything similar in England. There's the Queen and Prime Minister but their not passionately supported like here. Maybe because our lives are too comfortable, there isn't an opportunity for our leaders to lead and therefore be supported, if not worshipped. Moments in history have shown this to be the case when England's been under attack. What would've become of Churchill without the war?

Anyway I wonder how it feels to be mourned by so many.

The main factor in this cemetery being a tourist attraction is the tomb of Eva Peron. Each day hundreds of Argentinians and foreigners visit this tomb of the former president's wife. I wonder how she feels about this, whether she's happy that so many photos are taken of her final resting place, whether she wants to rest in peace in the midst of such hustle and bustle. It's a bit like the graffittied grave of Jim Morrison in Paris or the Lenin mausoleum in Moscow. Did they ask to be put there before dying or did their families decide after their deaths?

This got me thinking about how I'd like to be, preserved is the word I suppose, after my death. In one of these fancy tombs would be strange. I can't help feeling they should be for deserving figures that've done something good for the country or the world- like soldiers, doctors or campaigners. Not just some person from the public who wants one last expensive thing for all to look at and remember him by now he's no longer alive to drive his Porsche around.

Maybe I wouldn't want to be buried. Being stuck in the same spot for eternity with the same spirits, if that's how it goes, seems like hell. Maybe I could be cremated and have my ashes blown far and wide, all around. As long as they don't end up in a rubbish dump or a dirty canal.

But on the other hand I wouldn't like to be in one of these crumbly graves which look like part of the pavement. Though it would be more humble and in line with the majority of the rest of the world's dead. People who come across it would would wonder who lay there and wonder who I was, just like all graves. When you look at a random grave you don't know who that person was, what he did, if he worked hard for a living, if he showed his kids love. It's just a name, some figures and maybe a message. And there's another next door. And another next to that. All dearly beloved to some but nobody to most.

Unless you're Peron, Lenin or Jim Morrison in their Disneyland memorials. But then did they ask to be buried and remembered this way?

There's nothing they can do about it now.

Chapter Twenty Four

From the noise of the capital city I've travelled to the beach down the Atlantic coast at Mar de Plata for a couple of days of relaxation by the sea. And that's what I've got. Long, wide beaches of golden soft sand lie next to one another, caressed by the touch of the sea. For hours I lay in the basking light of the sun, letting it heat my body as I listen to the soothing sounds of the waves. At times it's only me and nature. Other times many people are around, playing games, listening to music, making music, drinking maté, the Argentinian pastime. When it gets too crowded I search for a more secluded spot. Sometimes I sit by the rocks which climb out from the sea, making piers almost. There you can hear nature's volume rise as the sea waves gather momentum and crash into the rocks, making a sound audible to everyone nearby and throwing white foamed seawater into the sky and then towards wherever it happens to land.

I've always loved the sounds and movements of the sea. It always feels so melodic and full of rhythm. I love the sound of the waves crashing in the Doors' song 'Riders on the Storm'. I dislike the song otherwise, but the intro with the waves is great. I just wish the rest of the song had this same natural atmospheric sound. Maybe someone could remake the song and actually do it on the beach with the waves live in the background. It would be difficult but with today's technology it's probably possible. Also for that matter a song in the park with birds singing overhead. That'd be good.

As a child I used to look out at the sea and wonder if it was like a conveyor belt, that the horizon line was the start and the shore was the end. The front wave would crash and then move back under the sea until it got to the back again. Then it would move back down the belt and eventually to the front again. And the same with the next wave. And the next... Of course I now know that's not true. Or it hasn't been discovered.

I also used to think that all waves were the same. Again like products on a conveyor belt, a production line. But now I know they're not. They're all different with varying heights, strength and colours. If you were painting the sea you couldn't just put down one slab of blue paint and call it the sea. You'd have to use lots of colours to show all the colours the sea has – not only its blues, but also its greens and yellows and purples. Like Monet did. And he was nearly blind, but he knew what was in front of him.

In Mar de Plata I'm staying in a hostel run by a German lad named Damien. He came over from Germany to travel and enjoyed the town so much he decided to stay. Now he surfs and does other beachside activities when free from the demands of the hostel. The hostel's very laid-back and easy-going, just as Damien had desired. This is the life he wants at this stage. He's more or less the same age as me and opines that now is the time to be doing such things, now rather than later when children, finance and other responsibilities arrive. He says he sometimes misses his home and family but not enough to make him go back just yet. He reminds me of the English expression, 'absence makes the heart grow fonder'. He says that people usually only use that when discussing loving relationships between a man and a woman, but for him it includes also his family and his hometown and homeland. When he eventually goes back he will appreciate it all more. Unless he enjoys Mar de Plata too much and meets a girl, I remind him.

"Possibly" he says, "But you'll never know if you do nothing. It's better to regret doing something than not doing something."

And with this I completely agreed and took it with me to ponder as I made my way back to the beach and its ocean view. Could I do the same as Damian has done? I've lived abroad before, teaching English for a few years. Many people told me I was brave for doing so and I never really understood why. For me it was quite simple, work and live as normal but in a different country. I always knew I could adapt to any great differences in the culture and food, etc, and that new friends would soon be made. Maybe it was this people thought made me brave. For them it'd be difficult and scary, whereas for me it was quite easy and simple. But now the thought of doing it feels anything but easy and simple. For different reasons than those above. Now it feels more difficult to leave my family behind. They always miss me when I'm gone; I think my mum even cries when I go away on holiday. And now there's an extra member, little Andrew. I'd rather not be on the side of the world while he's growing up and doing funny baby things.

But those responsibilities which may eventually stop me from doing such things are not too far around the corner. I'm getting older and they're getting closer. Now might be the time to squeeze in one last foreign adventure. It might not be now or never, but maybe now or don't know when or if. And this time instead of planning it beforehand, job, flat, etc, I might just throw a dart at a map, or open the atlas randomly. Until I land on somewhere I like obviously.

I'm spending the night walking along the pavement by the beach, watching the fishermen seemingly pass the time rather than catch anything. If I lived by water I'd spend a lot of time fishing. Aside from the actual activity you can get other things done – talk with your friends, eat, drink, smoke. You could bring a laptop down with you and do some work, or watch TV. You could bring a portable barbeque and cook the fish as you catch them. Sounds like fun to me. I just need to live by water. I could live by the Thames. Or following on from before I could move to somewhere on the coast or by a lake.

I find a space between the fishermen sufficient for me to believe it's just me and the sound of the sea again. I sit on a sea wall a few metres above some rocks. After a few minutes a dark figure stands close to me on my right hand side. A man stands tall, casting a shadow in the moonlight. He's dressed in a suit and nice looking shoes and what might be a panama hat, it's hard to tell in this light. In any case he's not dressed in typical beach wear, even if it is night. I look down and see a few men fishing from the rocks. They stand still, staring at the vast darkness in front of them. If it wasn't for the sound of the water you might not think there was anything there. The waves aren't pounding the rocks now. They're gently slapping them to a rhythmic beat, like a slow jazz beat. Tat – tat – tat. My eyes are starting to close; I could probably sleep here right now listening to it. It's so relaxing.

Realising this isn't the best place to spend the night, I pull myself up and jump on to the path beside the sea wall. I walk away, looking back at the ocean behind me, not knowing when I'll next see it. I turn into the road that leads to the hostel. Tat – tat – tat sounding further and further in the distance.

Chapter Twenty Five

I feel alone though I sit in a crowded room. People are passing me but I only have eyes for the litre bottle of beer in my hand. A band is playing on the small stage in front of me but my mind doesn't seem to want to hear them.

The hostel I'm staying in is having a party. A band's playing and everything's being filmed by two cameramen. They say they're recording a publicity film for the hostel. I've been asked a couple of times if I'd like to be a part of it but I declined. I just want to be a part of the background. It took me some persuading to even get me this far. My original plan for the night was to go out for some dinner and then back to the hostel to sleep. When heading for the exit I saw that everyone seemed to be having fun so I gave it a chance. Since then I've just sat in the corner with my beer and watched everyone have fun.

A girl comes over to me and holds out her empty glass. "Top me up." she says. Before I can consider whether I should or not, I already have. And she's gone back to her girlfriend huddle. I ponder what just happened. Is that the done thing over here? When your drink's finished you look for someone who's got more and you hold out your glass? Or maybe that's just her way of doing things. It saves her money I suppose. I'm spending lots of money on this trip, maybe I should try to do it too. I don't think it would go quite as well for me though. It's the kind of thing only girls can get away with. I'd just look like a poor alcoholic.

They stand by the bar, there are three of them I think, it's hard to tell who's with them and who's not. They're chatting, giggling, doing what girls do when they're together. One of them is faced towards me as is her position. I might be wrong but she seems to be looking straight at me. I might be wrong, she might be looking at something behind me, or maybe she really likes the look of the sofa I'm sitting on. She doesn't seem too involved in the conversation with her friends. Only infrequently does she look back at them and nod or shake her head. By the looks of things she hasn't said anything the whole time I've been looking. Her mouth's broken into a smile and a laugh a few times but I don't think it's moved in a speaking motion. Whatever that is.

Just then the girls break into simultaneous laughter. It's audible over the music and the other conversations. The girls look around a little self-consciously; probably aware of the attention they've attracted, and then break into a smaller and quieter giggle. The three of them then look at me. The one who I wasn't sure about before (who I'll from now on refer to as the long-haired one) now definitely is looking. Our eyes have locked and for a second her eyes are all I can see. But a second is all it lasts, as she looks away, emotionless, no smile, nothing. Another girl looking is one whose face was obscured before. She looks at me and then back at the others before giving out another little giggle.

Are they all laughing at me? Did they see me walk in and decide I was the one they were going to have fun with tonight?

The third is the one who I gave the beer to (the short-haired girl from here on in). She looks over at me, laughing gently, until her laughter becomes a small smile. She takes a sip from her glass, smiles again and then returns to her friends.

I sit back and take a swig from the bottle, from what remains of it. Do I have another or should I go out for dinner now? The party seems to be heading towards its end. On the other hand that drink has loosened me up somewhat. I'm on holiday, I should relax.

I get up and make my way over to the bar, passing the girls along the way. The long-haired one watches my steps as I pass. I walk behind the other one, as walking any other way would take me away from the direction of the bar. I see her watching me out of the corner of her eye. Out of the corner of my eye, as I order another beer, I see them huddle together again, whispering and casting tiny glances towards me. My beer arrives and I wonder if I should stay here and make conversation with them. What would I talk to them about is the first issue to wonder. Then I wonder if I'd be able to maintain a conversation with them, my Spanish isn't great and they might not speak English. I decide to sit back down. I keep the corners of my eyes open so as to catch any reactions, of which there are none. Maybe I was just their subject of amusement. Or maybe I was nothing at all to them, just another face in the crowd. I see them drink up their drinks and disappear out of view.

I feel like a cigarette now. I think it'd help me relax. I bought a packet earlier today pretty much because they were so cheap. I thought I might as well take advantage. Now I just need a light. Maybe I can do like that girl and approach someone with my fag in my mouth and say, "Hit me." or "Light me up." or anything else that sounds ridiculous. "Come on baby, light my fire." maybe. Instead I simply ask the first person I see smoking, "Do you have a light?" And it's a boy too, so in any case I couldn't have used the other lines and then reasoned that I was being flirtatious in an ironic cheesy way. He gives me the light, no problem. But then he says that in Argentina it's customary to give someone a cigarette when you borrow their lighter. In an effort to save face I tell him it's the same in England and hand one over. I go back to my seat before anyone takes anything else from me. The hostel owner might take my shoes because I've walked on his floor in them.

Just after sitting back down I hear a voice bellow in my left ear.

"Hola!" I see the three girls from before sitting themselves down on the sofa perpendicular to mine. "Can we sit here?"

I nod, seeing that they're already sitting. And they asked in Spanish if you're interested.

"My name is Julia and this is Elena and Mariela."

Julia's the long-haired one, Mariela the short-haired one and Elena the other, not quite looking like she wants to be here.

"What's your name?" asks Julia, quite loudly it must be said. I don't think she realises just how loud she sounds. Looking into her eyes, she seems tipsy, bordering on drunk. I've known girls before whose volume goes up to 11 when they've had a few.

"Doug. My name's Doug."

They say something inaudible to each other. Maybe they didn't hear properly.

"Doug, like Diego."

"Aaaah." They all say.

As opposed to her friend, Mariela seems more sober and in general a quieter personality, shy or nervous even.

"What are you doing in Argentina?" asks Julia, the spokesperson apparently.

"I'm here on holiday. Travelling through the country."

"Do you like Argentina?"

"Yeah, it's nice. What's not to like?"

It's been Julia who's done all the talking so far. She seems very forward. Mariela is sitting quietly, seemingly taking it all in, nodding and half-smiling at my replies. Julia directs another question at me.

"What do you think of Argentinian girls?"

I know what she's getting at but I still want her to tell me.

"What do I think of them?"

"Yes." she nods. "Do you think they're pretty?"

There we go, much more to the point.

"Yeah, they're very pretty. I've liked what I've seen so far." I drink from my glass upon completing the sentence so as not to follow it with awkward staring.

Julia nods at my answer. You know how sometimes you just nod at what someone says but have nothing to say about it yourself. Then she looks over to Mariela to gauge her reaction. As do I.

During the last minute Mariela has been rolling a cigarette whilst listening to us. Now she looks at the finished rolled one and then at me with a smirk. She knows we're both looking for her reaction. Then she lies back against the back of the sofa and lights up the cigarette, her eyes fixed on mine and not moving an inch.

I'm honestly not sure which one I should be devoting my time to. Julia's doing all the talking but it's Mariela giving me the eye, as some call it.

After about five minutes the decision is made for me.

Chapter Twenty Six

After another five minutes or so of talking, Julia and Elena stand up and announce that they're leaving. "Enjoy your stay in Argentina." Julia tells me and gives me a hug. "Adios" says Elena and also hugs me. They then turn to Mariela and give her their goodbyes. They make their way to the door but not before wishing Mariela good luck.

And that leaves just the two of us. I can't help thinking this has been the plan all along. Not that I'm complaining.

We move from the bar area to the hallway by the front door. The band's stopped playing now and are tidying up their equipment. I stand opposite Mariela who stands back casually against the wall. Her right arm lies by her side, cigarette in hand at an angle so the smoke doesn't affect us. Her left hand moves through her black hair as she speaks, pushing it back, twisting the ends, putting it behind her ear. She looks like she's posing for an album cover photo or some kind of publicity shot. She brings the cigarette up to her lips, her moist red lips. She takes a puff before tilting her head upwards, gently opening her mouth and blowing out the smoke. Then she licks her lips to remoisten them.

Her beauty is all I can see in front of me. And all I can think about is her beauty. I try to listen to what she's saying but it's hard to concentrate, she's got me on a string. Her magnetism is pulling me towards her. I should concentrate more on what she's saying, the conversation's taken a more serious tone and she's telling me things that I should be paying attention to.

She tells me all about the boy who she loves but can't have. They were together until five years ago but she slept with someone else and it ended. Now her heart yearns for him and he refuses to listen to her pleas. She says he doesn't even acknowledge her.

"I see him around town all the time but he just ignores me. He walks the other way or pretends he doesn't see me."

I suggest to her that she should possibly try to forget about him, or at least give him some time and space to gather his feelings.

"Yes, I know." she agrees "I'm trying. I try to forget about him, to not think about him, but it's hard. I know it's not fair on my boyfriend but I can't help how I feel."

She looks down at the ground, sad seemingly at what she's telling me. Torn apart inside by the torment of her life. Myself, I'm trying to figure out if she just said she has a boyfriend as well as 'the love of her life.'

"Yes, I have a boyfriend. As you say, I need to move on, to make other plans. But I still love the other guy. My first love."

"And your boyfriend, do you love him?"

"Do you not think it's possible to love two people?" she asks me with a quizzing look, challenging me to tell her no. "I love my boyfriend. He's always there for me and we have a great time together. I need him too. I can't be by myself, I need someone to love me and take care of me."

She sounds sincere and honest. Her challenging look has disappeared; she seems to be saying it because she feels it. But then I see her face drop and eyes look to the ground as she tells me, "But my heart also belongs to the other guy, who won't have me. And I need someone. If I had no one then I'd probably kill myself."

"But why? Isn't that a little drastic?"

"Is it?"

"Yeah. You shouldn't say you're going to kill yourself, there's always a way out. Even if things don't work out with either of these guys, you can still find someone else. There's plenty of time for that."

She nods like she agrees with me or at least understands me. Then she opens her mouth but no words come out. She looks to the side, her lips slowly moving like she's mumbling to herself, practising what she'll say.

"I know for sure I don't want to grow old. I don't want to have lines on my face and my body looking unattractive. And I definitely don't want children." she puts a finger in her mouth, chewing the end of the nail. "If I don't want to live through those times, if I want to die before then, why not die now?"

I look at her thinking she's a little crazy and she looks at me like I'm completely stupid or naïve. It's a standoff. Maybe we need a third party to decide who's right.

I now start to think my single role for tonight will be to listen to her problems and possibly act as a kind of therapist. If she already has two lovers this is probably the only space remaining for me. I don't really think that's how I want to spend my night. I might prefer to spend it alone thinking about my own problems.

"I just don't think I'll ever really be happy. Ever." she breaks the silence. "There's always a part of me that wants something else, or that wants to escape. Maybe that's why I have affairs."

She has affairs too? Why's that? I put to her my curiosity.

"I…" she struggles to answer. She lifts her hands in front of her and shakes her head as if I've just asked her to calculate 4242 x 7787. "I like sex." she says, the most logical answer I suppose. I look at her like it's not really an answer. Who doesn't like sex? She recognises this and realises she has to expand on her answer. "But I like sex with different men. I want to know how it feels with different men, to experiment. It's never the same."

That was a better answer, a lot more honest. She's very honest about things. I wonder if her boyfriend knows about these affairs.

"Some of them. But it's only sex I have with these guys, nothing more. There are no feelings involved. My heart stays where it is."

"Do you not feel guilty about cheating on your boyfriend?"

"But I'm not cheating. I already told you, I don't love these guys. I have sex with them but I love my boyfriend. It's different. There's a difference, you know?"

I do know. I've just never been brave enough to believe it and go through with it myself. She stares into my eyes; she's got the answer she was looking for.

"Look, you're English right, but you're here in Argentina and soon you'll be in Chile, no? And you've been to other countries too in your life and will do again, yeah?"

"Yeah."

"But you're still English, aren't you? And you still love England. Will that change if you enjoy other countries?"

"No."

"No. Because you love England and the others are just holidays, a temporary thing."

She still looks at me, gauging my reaction. I don't know where to look. I'm not comfortable with us staring at each other, no matter how beautiful her eyes. I look away to see what else is happening in the room. Everyone seems to be doing like us, though I doubt they're having the same discussion. Mariela realises she has no competition in the staring contest and begins to roll another cigarette.

We stand in silence for a minute or two. Her preparing the tobacco and paper, head softly bopping to the music. Me drinking my beer and debating what's next for tonight. I feel like going elsewhere. This has wet my appetite and I don't feel like toddling off to bed just yet. I'll ask Mariela if she wants to join me. If she says yes, then good. If she says no, then fine.

"Do you want to get out of here, to go somewhere else?"

"And do what?" she asks, eyes not moving from what's being created between her fingers and thumbs.

"We can have a nice drink somewhere. You know this city better than me."

"Aha, then what?"

"And we'd have a good time together." What does she want, a whole itinerary of the night?

"Then what?" lighting the finished cigarette, still not looking at me though.

143

"We could get something to eat too."

She takes a drag and smiles. "Would you kiss me then or would I have to wait even longer?"

At least that's what I think she said. To be certain I ask her to repeat.

She moves towards me, her face centimetres from mine, still smiling. "At what point would you kiss me?"

Probably now I think to myself, unable to say it aloud as my mouth is now entwined with hers.

Chapter Twenty Seven

I lay on my back staring at the ceiling, unable to sleep. I feel uncomfortable in this bed, it's been a while since I shared one. The mattress is fine, there's just not much space for me. Mariela lies next to me, her legs spread from one side of the bed to the other. Her left leg's bent so the knee rests upon me, aimed at my crotch. Any sudden jolts from either of us will affect me more than her. She lies still and peaceful. Gently breathing in her sound sleep. I would be too if I could just manage to nod off. I'm shattered after the physical activity we've just performed, and so is Mariela by the looks of things. She put in as much effort as I did to make it a success. And a success it was. Definitely one to remember and saviour. A benchmark.

But now I lay here with my mind ticking over, trying to find something drab enough to send me to sleep. The option it chooses is something that's been on my mind almost ever since me and Mariela were left alone and started to speak seriously. Everything she told me about her boyfriend and the other boy she loves and the men she's had sex with, got me thinking that we're very similar in some ways. I was together with Michaela and loved her, yet I felt there was space somewhere in my heart for someone else. And as for the affairs, what she said about that is pretty much every man's wish so of course I feel the same way. But her general melancholic demeanour hit a chord with me. It felt very familiar and I sympathise with her for it. That's why I spoke up when she mentioned suicide. I've felt that bad too and I don't want someone else to do so as well. If I'm finding it hard to help myself I can try helping others in distress.

I'm still not sleeping and now I'm sad and thinking about stupid things. I should be thinking about the great sex I've just had and the pretty girl lying next to me.

I need to go to toilet now, time to get up. I know the door is in the opposite corner to the bed, it's just finding it in the dark could be a problem. I hope there are no obstacles blocking my path. I know there's a trail of clothes along the floor and it's there I begin to feel around in the hope of finding my boxer shorts. They were the last to come off so they should be close to the bed. And indeed they are. Unless they belong to one of her other male occupants of this bed. I manage to make my way out of the bedroom and to the bathroom without any trouble. On the way back I pass through the living room. On the coffee table to my left I see the bottle and two glasses of wine Mariela and I started to drink.

"You didn't drink much, I see." says a voice to my right, that of Julia standing in the doorway between the living room and kitchen.

"No, we didn't."

"You found something else to do?"

I nod shyly. At least that's what I intend.

"I wonder what that could've been."

My expression remains. She smiles, knowing full well I'm feeling a little uncomfortable.

"You know," she starts to walk towards me. "we had to decide which of us would go for you. Mariela won, so I had to leave you two to it. If you'd turned her down I would have had you."

She's standing right in front of me now. In fact our toes are touching. When she speaks I feel the air leaving her mouth touch my face. In a nice way. Not like when you get too close to your schoolteacher and their breath smells. This feels sexy. If the circumstances were different I'd be having sex with her too. No, let's be honest, if I was brave enough to have sex with her though her friend's in the room next door.

"You should go back." she says, and points with her head towards Mariela's room.

"Yeah." I start to walk away.

"But first," she grabs my arm and pulls me back towards her. "I want to know how it feels to kiss an English guy."

She plants her lips around mine and her tongue in my mouth. Her hands pull and pinch the skin of my bare chest. Then she lets me go before licking her lips. She turns and heads towards the kitchen, seductively moving her arse as she does.

"Chau lindo." she says and closes the door.

Chapter Twenty Eight

It's morning now and I've turned myself away from the comfort of Mariela and her bed. I have a short time to make it to the bus station. Today I'm crossing the border into Chile. I don't like rushing like this, especially when abroad. I woke up in the knowledge that I had plenty of time but Mariela and I lay in her bed talking about this and doing that. We finally pulled ourselves out of bed and to the front door, me missing out on breakfast because of the hurry. Never mind, I got other benefits out of it. We stood in the open doorway saying our goodbyes, embracing one last time, when Mariela began to kiss and nibble the side of my neck. I stood entranced, enjoying the feeling, gazing into the distance. It was then I noticed Julia standing in the kitchen watching us say our goodbyes. She stood leaning against the worktop with one leg cocked up clutching a mug of coffee. Once she'd seen me notice her she took one hand away from the mug and waved at me. Then she blew me a kiss. At exactly the same time Mariela raised her head from my neck. Her face awaited some kind of reaction from me, an expression of thanks for the act she'd just performed. I smiled. Not so intentionally, it just happened. I smiled at Mariela and then I looked over to Julia and smiled at her too.

"Bye Julia." I said.

"Bye Doug." she answered. By now one hand was rested on her hip.

"Bye Mariela." I said and gave her one last kiss.

"Bye Doug." she said.

I stepped out the door and she closed it and that was that. A good time was had by all but all parties must come to an end sometime.

Chapter Twenty Nine

It turned out to be a good night in the end, and it's that feeling that's got me walking on sunshine, or some other cliché line. Now I'm almost at the bus station and I'm doing alright for time. According to my map I'll cut out some time if I go through this square. This square with the ten or so drunken vagrants hanging around the benches. They don't seem too threatening. If I walk down this path and not the one directly next to them, I should be fine.

I can see one has moved away from the group and seems to be dancing. In any case he seems happy and not likely to cause trouble. Another stands close to him, not dancing, I'm not really sure what he's doing. He just seems to be standing next to the dancing old man instead of the rest of the group. The old man sees me approaching them. He smiles and nods his head, which I take to be a salutation gesture. The other, a lot younger, turns round and walks towards me.

"Give me a peso!" he says.

You get quite used to being asked for loose change when abroad. Sometimes I give some, sometimes I don't. This time I'm not going to. I'm not certain as to where my change is exactly, plus I'm short of time for making it to the bus station.

"No, sorry." I tell him. I often feel guilty in this situation but not so much today. He, and the group for that matter, don't seem to be here to beg for money. They look like a bunch of men out drinking in a town square. Probably continuing from the night before. If I hadn't come along, he wouldn't have felt the need of a peso.

Yet still he orders me to give him one. This is strange. Usually you're only asked once, even if you refuse. The only times they persist is when they mug you. Now he's asked again, and a little more forceful too. Again I tell him 'No.'

Now I can hear his friends calling him back over to their bench. They're too far away for me to hear exactly what they're saying, but by the sounds and tones of their voices they want him to return to them without robbing me of all I have.

He turns back to them. Unfortunately I can't see the expression on his face as he does. He only looks back for a second before looking back at me and telling me again to give him some money. This time he's put one leg in front of my leg closest to him so as to hinder my escape. He's also put one hand on the strap of my backpack on my right shoulder. He's getting serious. I look up at his face. He's young-looking. He doesn't look homeless, or in great need of my money. He just looks like he's had a good night out and is continuing the fun, which makes it strange and difficult to understand why he's getting threatening now. I thought he just wanted to play 'let's have fun with the foreigner'.

"Give me a peso!" he tells me again. "Or I'll take everything." and he shakes the strap with his hand to illustrate the point.

"No!" I tell him forcefully and move my shoulder free of his hand. I'd like to give him a shove but I think it best to keep my hands in my pockets, there where my wallet and passport are. As long as my hands are in there, he can't get to them.

"Give me a peso or I'll take everything!" he repeats.

What do I do now? I think back to the last time I was in such a position, the time with Michaela back in London when I calmly reasoned with him. I wonder if I should do that now, though it would be much harder to do so in Spanish. Plus, if I spend that much time, energy and brainpower on doing that then I might as well locate my change and give him a peso. How much is it worth to me? About 15p I think. And that's what bothers me. Why is he getting so aggressive over 15p? If he was demanding I give him my wallet then I'd at least understand. No, the point is that he wants some fun with me and wants to frighten me. I'm not frightened, but I am beginning to get angry. My happy post-sex mood is disappearing thanks to this fool. I'm now slowly starting to feel a dark mist gather around me.

From the previous mugging attempt I also remember Michaela scolding me afterwards for not being aggressive enough. Until now I haven't thought about what I would do if something happened again. I suppose it was a matter of time before I was put into such a position again. Do I need to kick some lumps out of him to prove a point to Michaela? To prove a point to myself? I don't know. I do know I don't want to be made a mug of. Do I do this by walking away or by fighting him?

I remind myself that I never actually beat blood out of anybody. Not Adam, not the boy outside the pub, nobody. Perhaps now's the time.

I feel his leg jab ever more into mine. The whole time it's been there blocking my legs from moving forwards, but now it's pressing mine backwards. This guy's starting to make the decision for me. I shove him in the gut with my elbow and try to step over his leg. He pulls harder on my strap, pulling me back and halting any progress I'd made.

"Go away!" I tell him. His final warning, I say to myself. I clench my right fist inside my pocket should he not heed it.

It's then that his friend comes over to see what the commotion's about. He immediately drags him away by the arm, a bit like a parent does to a child who won't come inside from playing in the garden.

Dragging my would-be mugger with one arm, he raises the other in a diplomatic manner. "Sorry amigo." I hear him say and he smiles embarrassingly at the behaviour of his friend.

I stand and watch the two of them return to their group. After a few metres the older one lets go of the other's arm and they peacefully walk side by side until they reach their friends and rejoin the banter. I'm not sure the others even realise they were gone. No one seems to be talking about it, not even my would-be mugger. I don't think it matters to him much at all that I refused to give him anything. He only wanted some fun, to play on the supposed fact that he could get something should he want to. It didn't matter if he got 1 peso, 10 pesos or everything in my bag, he just liked the idea of doing it.

I walk away feeling strange, bemused maybe, at what just happened. I'm peeved that I've got myself so worked up over what this lad's done. Since my incident and stay in hospital I've felt reasonably calm and stress-free, if not always so happy. I've felt no need to get angry with anyone, or even contemplate fighting them in order to prove that I can. But now in one moment it's all come back and I'm not sure on what side of the fence I'm to stand. It's made me think about what's in England and what awaits me there when I return. Suddenly my holiday's full of reminders of home.

Chapter Thirty

Despite my delay en route to the bus station I still manage to arrive with time to spare. I find my seat and rest my head against the window in the hope of sleeping for the majority of the journey. My eyes flicker and I doze in and out of slumber for I don't know how long. Whenever I try to sleep during the day I always begin with short surreal dreams. This time images of Mariela and what happened last night are interspersed with other clips that I can't quite pin down or recognise. In one I seem to be in the sea, my head bobbing under and above water. When I go under I only see blue. When I go above I see a man sitting a few metres away. He seems to be sitting on top of the sea, on a stool beside a table maybe. Or a piano perhaps. It's difficult to tell, as soon as I begin to gather my thoughts, my eyes open and I feel the power of the bus engine.

After a period I'm able to quickly close my eyes and nod off again but this time the bus driver makes an announcement about something and this time I find myself unable to slip away to my subconscious. Sensing my inability to drift back to sleep, the passenger in the seat next to me begins a conversation.

"Where are you from my friend?"

I glance over to make sure he is in fact speaking to me. He sits emotionless, looking straight ahead, towards the front window and the driver. He might not be speaking to me, but it seems more likely than him just speaking to thin air.

"I'm from England." I answer.

His face and head remain in the same position, though now he's nodding a little. I expect a further question to prolong the conversation but there isn't one. There's only dead air.

After about two minutes he breaks the silence. Still looking straight ahead, he asks me if I've enjoyed my stay in Argentina.

"Yes I have. Very much so."

"And how have you found the Argentinian people?"

"On the whole," I consider my words carefully, "they've been nice. Friendly and welcoming."

He smiles and turns his head towards me, "Really?" he sounds surprised.

I wonder if there's anything I should or could add. I think of the locals I've encountered. As I said they've been generally nice, friendly and welcoming. Mariela was an extreme in one direction and the guy in the square this morning was an extreme the other way. I decide to stick to my original answer.

"Yeah, they're nice people."

He turns his head back to where it was, smirking a little at my answer.

"You haven't had any problems with anybody? You haven't been threatened?"

"No, not really. I'm sure not everyone I met is perfect but generally they seemed like good people."

I'm a little taken aback by his question. Where does he think I've been? I wonder what he's going to ask me next.

Now he looks at me, staring in fact.

"But didn't you ever feel that the behaviour of the people annoyed you? The volume at which they speak, for example. Or their lack of manners or etiquette." he pauses. "Their constant tooting of their car horns gets me. Makes me so mad."

These things have in fact come to my mind at times during my stay, particularly in Buenos Aires. It's actually been apparent to me that people here aren't bothered or upset by whatever impoliteness or bad manners or whatever it is you can call it. Ok, I'm sure if there was an extreme case then someone would speak up but on a normal basis I believe most people just shrug their shoulders and dismiss it. I think there's a lesson for people in that. And for me especially considering what happened this morning.

"I did notice those things but I can't say that they annoyed me that much. They were just things to get used to I think."

"I think of all the people I've come across the Argentinians are the most emotional. Their emotions and feelings dictate their actions and behaviour. For better or worse."

"Aha." I suppose.

I wonder if some emotion could dictate his voice, it's so monotonous. I'll soon be asleep again I think. I should probably keep the conversation going, out of politeness.

"And where are you from?"

I see that small smile on the side of his mouth again.

"I've lived in a variety of places, but most recently I've called Chile home."

The noise on the bus suddenly stops which probably means only one thing, the engine's been switched off. Looking out of the window at the still landscape confirms for me that the bus has halted. We're already at our first stop. We must've been talking for longer than I'd imagined.

"Ok, this is my stop. Have a very pleasant journey, enjoy it. Your life is still young and fragile, cherish it and make good use of it."

He then turns and walks away towards the exit at the front of the bus. Leaving behind some old man wisdom.

Once again I lean my head against the window, this time to get a glimpse at who my next travelling companion could be.

Chapter Thirty One

As it turns out only a handful board the bus and not one of them joins me. I can't say I'm too disappointed. A little time without disturbance is what I require just now. Not that it's helping me with my desire to sleep. That looks like a lost battle.

Instead I turn my attention to the view outside the window. Portraits of landscape beauty flow past me, each one full of the magical touch of nature's palette. I see rugged, sandy land broken up by tranquil turquoise lakes. I see rocks that appear untouched and unmoved for perhaps centuries. In the distance I see hills disguising the horizon, the mid-afternoon light illuminating them in a shade of lilac. Above them a thin dim of cloud has gathered, hiding the body of the mountains. At the top of my window-framed picture I can see the remains of the winter snow sprinkled upon the mountain tops. Views from roads don't get much better than this. I shall remember this the next time I'm on a bus in London.

The bus conductor walks up and down the aisle to inform us of the Aconcagua mountain in view on the right side of the bus. Aconcagua's the tallest mountain in South America and I believe one of the top 3 in the world. I can see it now in the space between the mountains. At this proximity it doesn't look so high. Or not much higher than the others I should probably say. I wonder if I could reach the summit. Great peaks such as this one are there to be conquered, and have been many times. It'd a challenge of strength and stamina, and also commitment. It's the last bit that bothers me the most. I doubt I could put in all the necessary training and preparation. I'd probably need to go to the gym for a year to get myself ready and at some point there's a strong chance I'll question what the hell I'm doing.

As I hesitantly pencil in a near 7000m climb onto my to-do-before-I-die list, I notice the road get thinner and more winding as we pass through the mountains that make up the Andes. If climbing a mountain seems too daunting then what about trekking through the range? I've trekked many times before, it's something I enjoy and usually do well. It doesn't involve so much fitness or training seeing as it is the training and it's making you fit. Could I trek through this same path the bus is taking me? It's reasonably flat, that's the plus that strikes me right away. It'd be a bit of a stroll, a very scenic stroll. Or a series of strolls. On the bus it's taking about 5 hours, on foot it would take… longer, I conclude. I'd have to camp out overnight, several nights, in the middle of nowhere, with all kinds of animals and creatures around me. It'd be a test of survival I think. Like those training missions the SAS get sent on. 'If you don't make it back alive, don't come back at all.' But I feel I need some kind of physical challenge. I'm on holiday spending my whole time sitting. Sitting in towns, sitting on beaches, sitting in cafes, sitting in bars, sitting on buses. Ok I'm on holiday, I should relax. But I shouldn't be so lazy.

After starting to think about whether I could come back this way to trek later on, something puts me off the idea. In fact something makes me think that sitting and sitting very still would be a great thing to do. After winding ever upwards through the mountain pass, it's now time to drive back down to something closer to sea level. A glimpse out of the right window shows me the road ahead – a road bending like a coiled up snake all the way down the mountain. We start our descent and it feels like a slow rollercoaster. We drive to the end of the first stretch, about 30-40 metres I guess, follow the road down and around to the right, leading to the next stretch below. The same pattern follows. This time the view on my right shows me the buses and trucks following us. Each one moving as slowly and safely as the next, as if they were driving on a tightrope. We reach the end of the second stretch and turn left. Two down and I think I can now count ten to go.

Looking out of the window now I can see that the bus is driving less than one metre from the edge of the road. My mind fills with possible reasons for us falling. Perhaps a bird or a fly will obscure the vision of the driver, or a sudden noise will distract him, or maybe dust will infect his eye. That could happen, there's a lot of sand around. He could sneeze even. I wonder if the drivers are specially trained for this. Do they have special tests to pass? Do they have to keep their windows closed so no dust or flies can enter? Is the driver area sound proof? Do they have to practice driving along a piece of string? If I'd known we'd be confronted with this road I possibly would have asked the driver a few questions before boarding. For example, when did you last drink alcohol?

All that being said, this guy's doing well. He probably passes through here a few times a week. In any case, he's filling me with confidence. However, I do decide to take my mind and my eyes away from the road. Instead I look above to the mountains surrounding us. Looking up at the peaks I can see snow, but as we descend the mountains stand next to what look like giant piles of stones and rocks. It's these piles that surround the snake road we're driving. Only they're not really piles. Except in the sense that these piles begin from the top and are building downwards instead of up. I can see lines of rocks suspended at an angle, resting on these hills. If one moves, then the rest do and all the traffic on this road will suddenly be moving a lot quicker. Again I consider the possibilities. No birds or flies could do anything. For a few moments I ponder whether the wind could move any of them. Then it finally dawns on me. An earthquake. We're in an earthquake zone, one could hit at any time. Imagine if someone was on this bus on this road during an earthquake. I wouldn't like the chances of survival. Nature wouldn't wait to let the traffic pass. When it's time for the ground to open up, it's time.

Fortunately we've almost made it to the bottom. Though it does occur to me that that's not too much consolation. Even at the bottom an earthquake would send all those rocks down towards and possibly onto me. I could be nowhere near the mountains, on the beach for example, and an earthquake could kill me. Or in bed or walking in a park. At any given time the ground could open and swallow me whole. Or something could fall from the sky and bury me underneath it. I'd never really thought about it before now. Now I suspect it's going to be filling my thoughts a lot more often.

The bus leaves the final bend and the road widens as it straightens out again. Looking ahead now the descent from the mountains appears to be a more gradual one. I feel the engine of the bus rev an extra notch and step up a gear. I sit back and close my eyes, feeling the need to relax again and stop worrying about matters out of my control.

Chapter Thirty Two

The bus crossed the border into Chile without problems, no earthquakes, no collisions on thin mountain roads, no falling debris. I'm in a town that was built inside a national park about 10 years ago. I say town, but it's a few roads joined together dotted with hostels, restaurants and a few shops. The basic things a tourist needs in this kind of place. Walking around makes me think of those small towns you see in films where everyone knows each other and knows everything about each other. It must be like that here. I guess there are barely more than a hundred people who live here.

I see a sign in a window that says, 'Baker wanted'. It seems interesting to me. I wouldn't want to work as a baker, and they would do well not to hire me, but could I work here in any capacity? Could I survive in such a small community? It could get quite tiresome I can imagine, seeing the same faces everyday, but then there are always the beautiful mountains to disappear to when a break feels necessary.

So that place is looking for a baker. I'll keep my eye out for other vacancies. An English teaching job would be ideal.

I wonder how things were here when the town was first created. When the first inhabitants arrived, were they assigned jobs and homes by a body? Maybe there was a lottery or some kind of contest. Judging by the glum faces on the boys working in the supermarket, they lost.

I notice there's no church to be found. Not even a makeshift hut. Is this an atheist town? Or maybe no one's realised. They all thought someone else was building the church. I wonder what God makes of that. Maybe he hasn't noticed. Or maybe he's building his rage as I write this.

That's a little unfair. People always think God's angry when his word or will isn't followed. But who knows? It's all opinion. And I've got my own.
I think God gets quite a harsh deal nowadays. Most of the time he gets the blame for everything that goes wrong. Ok, he did create everything but maybe God just wasn't a great planner. He didn't think everything through. Maybe he had a deadline to meet and he rushed it. And these fancy creations never look as good in reality as they do in your head.

Is this even how God had planned it in the first place?

Does anyone even pay attention to him now? Maybe just the Italians and Irish. I think for everyone else it's only when they want something. It is for me that's for sure. That must be depressing, sitting up there looking down on your creation, pulling your hair out at how badly it's going, the people down there ignoring you, only wanting you when they need something. I think more people should put themselves in God's shoes. How would they feel if it was them? And remember, God is cool. All the cool things you like were invented by God. Ok, and the rubbish things too. But imagine what other inventions lie ahead, waiting to be discovered. I bet God invented the Internet centuries ago but man wasn't smart enough to discover it or work it out. The same for sliced bread. I reckon the alternative to oil has been under our noses all this time, we just haven't realised.

Anyway there's no church in this town, which could be a good thing. In those films of the small towns there often seemed to be a murderous cult linked to the churches so I should probably be grateful no one's trying to kill me here.

All this time spent in urban areas and viewing the countryside from a bus has fuelled my desire to get out there and experience nature for myself. There's no point thinking about walking through mountain passes and vast open fields if you're never going to do it. I could be dead tomorrow so I'm going to do it today; no threat of earthquakes, tsunamis or muggers is going to stop me.

There's a peak inside this park that can be reached following a few hours trek. This should go a long way to at least partially fulfilling my desire. It's not necessary to climb to the summit of Aconcagua to give yourself some exercise and get your energy flowing.

I approach the entrance to the trail sceptical as to whether I'll even be able to try to go to the summit. It's a grey and cloudy morning, very cloudy in fact. The clouds are so low I can't even see the summit. To be honest I don't even know which hill it is I want to conquer. I reach the trail's beginning where the park ranger awaits me. He plays down any fears of danger, only advising me on the length of time I should aim for when ascending. I ask him at what time the cloud will lift and he says something about not seeing the weather forecast this morning. How can he be so confident that everything will be fine up there? Are there floodlights at the top underneath the blanket of clouds? He gives me a map and tells me which signposts I need to pay attention to. 'Come on Doug!', I tell myself. 'don't wimp out now. Remember, don't let anything stop you. Carpe diem!' I head off to begin the trek, my mind wondering if 'Carpe diem' is the correct Latin phrase. I mean something like, 'Grab the day.' or 'Capture the day.' or 'Don't put off until tomorrow what you can do today.'

The trek begins with a nice walk through a dark forest. The gradient is only slight so I don't feel any problems yet, it's almost a gentle stroll. The trees are tall and reasonably thick, but it's not a dense forest. It's not essential that I follow this path, there's plenty of space around to meander. Looking up above, the leaves on the trees are plentiful and green. They almost appear to be joining from one tree to the other, forming a canopy or roof of sorts. I had hoped to catch some sun today whilst walking but the forest and clouds might have ended those plans.

Suddenly I can hear the sound of flowing water and true enough the path leads me to a stream. It's only small and shallow and of no great use. Luckily the trek's just begun and I have enough water in supply. To cross the stream I must pass a tiny bridge made up of a log lying from one bank to the other. Easier than it perhaps looks. Even if I fell from the log I wouldn't be left in too much danger. The drop is less than a metre high and the water not deep enough to drown a mouse. I take two steps on the log and walk along the opposite bank. Up ahead I can see where the path is heading.

For about an hour I climb a thin steep trail leaving the forest and leading into woods. I clear branches blocking not only my path but also my view. It's getting more and more difficult to see now. I push away one branch like pushing open a door but am then confronted by another. And another. For a short while I imagine an enemy or pursuer of some sort is walking directly behind me and gets whacked by a branch each time it swings back after me moving it. That fun only lasts for a short while though, as I soon get agitated and tired of these branches and what's on them. Some of them have flies or insects on them which then climb on to me and others have spider webs. The flies and insects aren't quite so bad seeing as a quick swat usually gets rid of them. The webs on the other hand are more difficult and irritating. I can see strands of web glisten in the light, though that still doesn't make them any more comfortable or nicer on my skin or in my hair.

I'm walking quicker and quicker now in order to escape this web ordeal. It only occurs to me now that I'll have to come this same way on the way down.
'I hate nature!' is the phrase I have in my head. I remember a scene from the film 'The Goonies' when Chunk is escaping from the baddies through the woods and he says over and over, 'I hate nature!' I'm coming to that same opinion. I had such a hunger to come here yesterday and thought that nature looked so beautiful. Now that I'm among it I feel very different. Maybe I think nature is only beautiful from afar.

I've now reached a wooden signpost in the trail. To continue my route I must take the left path... the steep one. I take a look at the other just to see what I could have won. It's almost the same as the one I've just left. The one I'm on now is steeper but wider and more open. I can already feel more light breaking through.

The quick pace I set before is now catching up with me. I can barely walk a few metres up this slope before needing to stop and rest. The water I have isn't going to last much longer at this rate. And I can really feel aches in my calves now. Each step feels like a climb as I haul myself up this slope. I remember my guidebook said something about its steep gradient but I doubt it'd be this much trouble for someone fitter than what I am. I knew I wasn't in great shape but this is showing me just how much I need to improve. I'm walking ever so slower now and am feeling twinges in my knees now as well.

For goodness sake I really am unfit. It's now a real strain to even put one leg in front of the other. I'll have to do something about this when I get home. And I'll do it properly this time, no attempts at a quick fix like before. I'll join a gym, do exercise when I get up in the morning and go running at night. And I'll have to be patient too; nothing's going to happen overnight.

Another part of my body's trying to tell me something now, my belly's rumbling and wants to be fed. That's fair enough I suppose; breakfast was a few hours ago now. In my bag I have some bread, oranges and a bar of chocolate. I'll stop to eat up ahead when I find a suitable spot. Everything at the moment's made up of bushes on the mountain side and tiny rocks on the other side, protecting me from the edge of the path and the drop below. Hopefully soon there'll be a rock big enough for me to sit on and rest. Lord knows I need it.

I probably shouldn't be so surprised that I'm struggling up this hill. I didn't have the biggest breakfast in the world and it has been a while since I've done anything like this. It was possibly too demanding to expect me to waltz up here without breaking sweat. But I've come this far and I'm not turning back, even though I can see the path rising again ahead of me. It rises so much that it stands above the tips of the enormous trees whose trunks I passed a few hundred metres down below. Now the scenes around me are clearing and I can get a glimpse of the view from where I am. I follow the path up, up and up until it suddenly flattens out and leads me to a plateau.

What strikes me immediately is the light. For so long I've been walking in the shade of the forest, with the only shining light being that which pierced through between the leaves above me. Now I'm in the open sunshine and above me is a clear blue sky.

I turn around to gaze at the view surrounding me. Down below I see green. The tops of the trees I've now left behind in my wake. Left behind, just like my tiredness and hunger. I've been given fresh impetus and inspiration, a natural high. Looking out ahead I see the clear blue sky hover above, not the land at the bottom of the mountains, but a sheet of white cloud. That same cloud which this morning threatened this expedition now lies under me, looking up at me for a change.

Chapter Thirty Three

Thankfully the plateau has several rocks to sit on. None are in shade however, so feeding my hunger has to wait further still while I put on some sun tan lotion. For the time being I only seek to protect my most attractive areas to the sun – my nose and the back of my neck. I'll do my arms and the rest of my face after I've eaten. I dig out my little plastic bag of food from my rucksack and tuck in. Never before has plain bread tasted so good.

Whilst eating I look over the clouds once more. They look like a blanket of ice cream or marshmallow. I want to dive on to them and use them like a bouncy castle. I've seen the clouds like this before of course when on an aeroplane, but this is different. I'm not looking at them through a window or from a confined space.

After a feeling of near claustrophobia among the leaves, branches and webs all touching me, after almost being hidden and disguised by the trees, I now feel free and almost suspended in mid-air even.
In fact it occurs to me that no one can see me sitting up here. At the bottom I could barely see anything of the mountain because of the cloud. Now I'm above the cloud and can't see anything below it. It's something that intrigues me and fills me with fascination. It feels like I'm on top of the world. But then I think that this could work against me. I could fall or have any kind of accident and no one would know. I suppose the park ranger I met at the bottom would come looking for me at some point but who knows if it would be too late.

I peel an orange for an injection of vitamin C and prepare myself for the next step of my trek. I look behind me to where the trail leads. It's a wider path with next to no shade, at least for the beginning from what I see. It doesn't seem as steep as before and in any case I'm walking with renewed vigour and intensity. The path winds left and right up the mountain, taking me around random trees and bushes which would block a straight walk.

I start to hear a strange sound, a huge buzzing like a lawnmower or a chainsaw. This is a national park after all, so it could possibly be a workman doing maintenance on a tree. Or it could be a madman looking to recreate 'The Texas Chainsaw Massacre'. Again I'm reminded that no one will see me die up here. The noise is getting louder and closer, yet there's no sign of anybody or anything. I walk a bit further and pass a large upright bush on my right. It's there the noise is coming from. Bees I think to myself. There must be a bees nest inside the bush. By the sounds of it there has to be hundreds inside. I quickly walk away before they fly my way.

In my haste to abandon the nest I stumble on the ground and my foot kicks a small rock below me. Myself, I only slip back a few centimetres and am able to keep my balance by touching the ground with my fingers. The ground I'm walking now is more treacherous than before. In the forest the ground was covered in leaves from the previous autumn and winter. Now I'm walking on a sandy dirt track. There's little to grip my feet on, nor hold on to with my hands. That slip just now was a warning; it could be a lot worse. How do I know that all these rocks are stable? What if I use one as a step to pull myself up and it gives way? I could cause a rockslide. Or a landslide. Is there a difference? If I cause debris other than rocks to fall, is that a landslide? What if one of these rocks is a booby trap? This day out could turn out to be an Indiana Jones film with me ducking arrows and being chased by giant balls.

All of a sudden I don't feel as relaxed as I did before.

And it's getting hotter. Sweat is now dripping from my eyebrows and the tip of my nose. I wipe my forehead dry with my wrist and my wrist gets wet. And full of spider webs. Are they still on me? I really hope there's not a spider crawling around me somewhere. I can feel the sweat running the sun tan lotion off my skin and into my eyes. Aaah, that stings. I wipe them clean but my hands and fingers must have the same sweat/lotion mixture on them as my eyes sting more when they touch them. Quite a stupid thing to do. A bit like touching your eyes after chopping chilli. And now I hear more buzzing. It's not just a bee flying around me; it's a collective buzz, again like a nest. Please don't let them visit me. Let them just keep buzzing in their nests and I'll just walk on by minding my own business.

Over to my right I can see another small plateau. I begin to walk towards it when another round of buzzing stops me dead in my tracks. The path to the plateau splits between two bushes, both of which seem to have buzzing emanating from them. I decide to continue with my planned route. I doubt the view from there was much different to anything I've seen before anyway.

I slowly and carefully continue my way on the trail, keen to keep both my footing and keep the peace with the bees. After an hour or so the sandy path gives way to a path of rocks which I must negotiate to get any further. Again I think about rockslides. Huge rocks stand either side of the path now, framing it, separating it from the trees and bushes. Above me I can see the summit. I'm almost there. I feel good. I don't feel as tired as I did before. In fact I've felt better as I've gone on. Maybe I just needed to get used to walking in such conditions. It's still hot though and the sweat's still dripping off me. Sometimes I feel it enter my mouth, it

172

tastes salty. My biggest problem now is the weight I think I've lost while walking in this heat. My trousers are definitely looser than they were this morning.

I've made it, I've reached the top. Mission accomplished. It wasn't plain sailing, I had a lot of difficulties at times and felt like turning back, but I didn't. I just needed to overcome some mental issues and convince myself I could do it. And now I've made it. It might not seem a large achievement for some but for me it is. I needed to prove to myself that I could do this.

There's a plaque up here commemorating Charles Darwin's ascent 200 or so years ago. I wonder if he knew where he was going; there might not have been marked trails in those days. And I wonder if he had such problems concerning fitness, hunger, heat and bees. Or if his trousers also felt looser afterwards.

Chapter Thirty Four

It's the next morning now and I've woken early. Or I've been awoken early I should say. For I don't know how long I tried to sleep through the noise being generated outside my room but finally keeping my eyes closed and urging myself to sleep no longer worked. Clear as a bell, as if they were next to me, I can hear people shouting. Not aggressively like in an argument but just to communicate with each other. And I've no idea for how long they've been at it. Each wink of sleep I've captured could have lasted a minute or an hour, I don't know. Looking at my watch would've required more effort and would probably have led me to be permanently awake. Not that it matters now, there's no way I'm going to get back to sleep now. I might as well get up and start the day. I should check the time as well, you never know, I might've slept through breakfast.

No, it's ok, it's 9.30, half an hour left. It's not a bad time to get up, not too early nor too late. That doesn't mean I'm thankful to my fellow guests. 9.30 is still an early hour to be shouting like that. And like I say, who knows what time they started.

I rise out of the bed and look for some trousers to put on. I consider going out there in just my boxers to gain something like revenge on the noisy neighbours, but I don't want to be petty. I find a pair and put them on, looking around to see who's with me in this 8-bed dorm. Just one other guy it turns out. I'm careful to limit the noise of my zipping up my trousers. I make my way over to the door and open it, only to be surprised by someone standing directly on the other

174

side. He's alone and yelling loudly into his phone. Who knows why, he's not repeating anything so I doubt the person on the other line is having trouble hearing him. It just seems to be the way he speaks. As I close the dorm door behind me I put my index finger to my lips and then point inside the dorm. Then in case he still has no idea I put my two hands flat beside the right side of my head and close my eyes. If he didn't get it before, he's got it now. He takes a few steps down the corridor and continues his conversation there.

I walk towards the kitchen thinking about that. I didn't do it to be clever or righteous. It was intended to be better natured than that. Maybe the man doesn't know he speaks so loud. At least for people still sleeping. I handled it quite well I think, better than I would've done a few minutes ago when my beauty sleep was cut short. I enter the kitchen and surprisingly find it empty. Where has all the noise and its makers gone? I peek my head out into the corridor again and see a big group down by the reception. This time it's the young girl who works here in the middle of the eardrum banging. I go back into the kitchen, keen to make full use of the tranquillity while I can. I directly make my over to the crockery pile in the corner. This also made a racket earlier on, with cups and plates crashing on tables. I'm not going to be such an arsehole as to describe for you how I can pick up a mug without making a noise, but I manage to anyway. I pour myself some coffee out of the canister, and go on the lookout for some milk. In front of me I see a jug of white liquid that doesn't look like milk and a jar of white powder that doesn't look like milk either. I smell the liquid and swirl it around, discovering that it is in fact yoghurt. The powder, I'm still not sure of. Maybe this hostel

175

assumes everyone drinks their coffee black, I've nothing against it, I just prefer milk. But I start to drink it black nonetheless.

Next to the white powder I see a loaf of sliced bread. I put three slices of it into the toaster and eye up the different spreads – butter, jam and this sweet caramel/toffee one too. Still no sign of milk. Most hostels on my trip so far have offered a good hearty breakfast – bread, eggs, cereal, fruit. But here it's bread. I'll have to fill myself up on toast then, three will make a good start.

I sit with my coffee whilst I wait for my bread to toast. It's a small kitchen but they've still managed to accommodate two medium long tables. The walls are adorned with posters of the Chilean countryside and its wildlife. Others are campaigning for the preservation of the Chilean countryside, which with each passing year is coming under greater threat by big businesses with big axes, big bundles of dynamite and big cases of cash. This hostel promotes itself as green and eco-friendly. There are many tourists who come here with little or no idea of the dangers and threats to the natural beauties that they've come to visit. It's this hostel's mission to let them know about it and take some of the knowledge home with them.

Scattered around the walls are also homemade postcards, I suppose you'd call them, containing different stats and quotes concerning the destruction of the environment. It feels a little heavy for this time in the morning I must say. They're not the best things to read when trying to relax and eat. I wonder if the guests making noise in here before me paid any attention to what's on the walls. Maybe that's what they were debating.

"EH, DID YOU KNOW THAT PLACE WE VISITED THE OTHER DAY MIGHT NOT BE THERE IN A FEW YEARS?!"

"REALLY? WHY'S THAT?"

"I DON'T KNOW. MAYBE BECAUSE OF CLIMATE CHANGE. OR BECAUSE SOME COMPANY WANTS TO DESTROY IT. LET ME SEE WHAT THIS SAYS…"

"THAT'S SAD, IT WAS SO PRETTY."

"I CAN'T UNDERSTAND THE REST OF IT, MY SPANISH ISN'T THAT GOOD."

Myself, personally, didn't come to stay at this hostel because of its eco-friendliness. It was more out of the convenience of it being cheap. I assume that was others' reasons too.

Pop! goes the toaster and I see my toast leap up into view. Good, I'm starving. I spread some butter on them and then some jam, that'll do nicely. As I put back the jam jar I see a small notice behind it on the wall which reads, '2 slices of bread per person.' I look down at my plate hoping I picked up only 2 slices even though I wanted 3. My hope isn't fulfilled. I turn around to check I'm still alone and thankfully I am. I then quickly eat one of the slices as quickly as possible to remove any evidence of the crime. No one will ever know. Unless someone counts the number of slices and reports to the manager if there's an odd number. How could they know it was me? Maybe they'd lock the front door and interrogate everyone until the guilty person was found. Or they have video cameras checking upon us that we follow the rules.

In the toilets there are also small signs asking guests to only switch on lights when absolutely necessary and then reminding them to switch them off when leaving. I've gone to the toilet in the dark every time since I arrived, even during the night. For me during the night is a necessary time to switch on the light in the toilet but who knows if that's the case here. Maybe there's a camera in there watching. Or someone outside with one of those light detector things they use in cricket to check the amount of light.

There are also such signs concerning the amount of toilet paper used, but that goes along similar lines to that of the light.

I can't be the only one breaking the rules though, can I? Surely someone's left a light on, or used too much toilet paper. Or used a teaspoon to stir their coffee and a knife to spread their jam, like I just have, without considering the amount of water that'll be wasted to wash them. Like I said before, I think most people have come to stay here out of convenience. I haven't seen any eco-warrior types here. You know the ones.

I sit down with my coffee and toast and look around for any cameras on the ceiling or the walls. None. But that doesn't mean there aren't any at all. Maybe they're hidden in the kitchen utensils or behind the posters like in Scooby Doo. Actually the eyes of the vicuña in that poster do seem to be following me.

My scan for cameras leads me to another 'helpful hint' about the environment. This one says that powdered milk is just as healthy and nutritious as regular milk and is of no danger to animals. That must be what that powder in the jar is then.

Some of the other guests now approach this end of the corridor again, as noisy as ever. Unfortunately there aren't any signs asking them to shut the hell up.

Chapter Thirty Five

From the town I head to the coast. Due to the thinness of Chile you're never far away from the coast on one side or the mountains on the other. This is my first sighting of the Pacific Ocean. I'd like to tell you how different it looks to the Atlantic I saw in Argentina but that would be lying. I see no difference. In fact it looks just like the sea at Brighton or in Devon where I went as a kid.

Instead of spending my time on the beach with everyone else and their dogs, I decide to visit the giant sand dunes that stand over the beach and the urban land around it. These dunes must be a few hundred metres above the sea and yet they look very stable. Sand must have piled up here for centuries and now today here I stand upon it all looking out to the ocean.
Approaching the dune from that side gave me little warning of what was to come. In front of me I could only see a field of sand, like a beach without the sea.

179

Then as I walked across it I found deep ditches and what would be crevasses in a glacier. I ran down the side of one until the steep angle and texture of the surface brought me falling to the bottom. There, I lay on my back and looked at my footsteps printed in the sand. Then I watched the tiny grains of sand fall from each one, causing the minutest of landslides. I looked up at the sky and watched the clouds move. They came drifting past me, much like people in the world. They come and go. They live and die. I remain lying and into my head popped the thought of lying in an open grave, it had that feeling. I was surrounded not by earth but by sand, walls of which were standing high around and above me, possibly 6ft above me. Despite this it felt comfortable and relaxing. My interrupted night's sleep in the hostel had caught up with me and I could feel my eyes close as they looked up at the changing colours of the evening sun.

Now I sit at the top of the dune looking down its face to the beach way down below. I have a similar feeling to one I had yesterday on the mountain, as to whether anyone can see me up here. I look around and can't see anybody else on the dune. Down the bottom everyone looks tiny, as I suppose I would if anyone were to look up here.

I strongly feel this sensation of being alone. Not lonely, just alone, by myself. Me, the sand, the sea ahead of me and the open sky above me. No noise, no distractions, no inconvenience. It's rare for both me and my surroundings to be this calm and peaceful. And to mark it I begin to think about England. I don't know why, just something makes me think about my return home and what I'll do there once I return. First of all

I'll need a job. Probably to begin with I'll just look for something, anything, to pay the bills. But I can't let myself stay like that for too long. It's time to make plans and set my sights higher. I've always wanted to have my own cafe, plus there's the idea of a hostel. I could open an eco hostel in London like the one I'm staying at now. I grin to myself though I shouldn't. At least they're trying to do something about the environment, which is a lot lot more than what I'm doing.

Ok, a hostel or a café perhaps. But such commitments have always been something I've wanted for later in my life, once my mischievous shenanigans are over. Perhaps now could be the time to put it into action. I'm only getting older now and it'd be nice to have something to call mine.

But on the other hand, at some point I'll probably get those itchy feet again and the travel bug and will want to set off abroad again. Maybe I could set up the café abroad. Something else to ponder.

More questions creep into my thoughts, how will I behave when I get home? What will my outlook be once the stress of London life kicks in again? Will I get angry at everything and one that disgruntles me or will I be calm and let it slide off my back? What if no one else is as calm, shall I try to advise them or leave them to it?

I doubt I'll know these answers until I get home and am confronted by the situations. At least I've shown to myself that I'm not oblivious to what awaits me when I get home. That was the first step, and quite a big one, and that satisfies me.

In fact it's been a quite satisfactory day all round. I didn't get too worked up at the hostel this morning. Sure, I moaned a lot to myself but that was just moaning. I was tired. A while ago I'd have wanted to bang each of their heads together; today I just let it pass. It didn't matter enough.

Not even the lad who ruined my attempt at a nap. During the middle of the morning I went back to bed to try to get some sleep. I'd been trying for about 10 minutes and was about to make good progress when one of the lads I'm sharing the room with came in. With only my ears to recognise what he was doing, I could hear him tap his fingers on the side of the wardrobe for what was about 2 minutes but felt like forever. And he did nothing else but this. Tap, tap, tap! Like he was sitting at a piano. In his defence he might not have seen me but I doubt it.

I didn't do anything though. I just felt tetchy because of my tiredness. Another time I would've either done nothing and regretted it or wanted to beat him up and feel satisfied. This time I feel fine. It doesn't matter so much. Why should it? Even though it was the same lad who was in the room with me earlier when I met the guy on the phone on the other side of the door.

Yeah, it's not been a bad day at all. I've watched the world glow in front of me and have felt positive and optimistic, but now the sun's disappearing and the day's ending. I hope it will be sunny tomorrow.

I don't like the idea of making my way from this dune in the dark, time to go. I carefully walk across the sand when something surprises me and stops me in my tracks. Up ahead descending into one of the ditches of the dune I see the man from the bus I was on the other day. I only briefly saw the back of his head but I'm pretty sure it was him. He was wearing that same hat and I doubt there are many with those around here. I approach the ditch and am puzzled to look down and see no one. Where did he go? Down and then up again? I turn a circle but still don't see him; in fact I see nothing but the sand and the sky. I don't even see his footsteps.

Chapter Thirty Six

This morning I stepped on a bus in Santiago. The search for my reserved seat led me towards the back of the bus, almost completely separated from the other passengers. There I found a large reclining seat next to the window with an elderly lady sitting comfortably in it. She sat with her newspaper and didn't look away from it as I sat down in the seat beside her, hers presumably. I don't know if she realised I'd reserved that one. Or of she'd taken it on purpose for whatever reason. I didn't say anything because I didn't mind so much. I usually reserve the window seat because I like to not only look out the window, but also lean my head against it when relaxing. There'd be no views to look at on this journey because we were travelling at night. And as for the window acting as a head rest, I gave that luxury up as a gift to the lady, my good deed for the day. Also, another sign that such petty grievances don't affect me as much now. Even though my sitting in the aisle seat meant that I had to let her pass each time she wanted to get up and go to the toilet, of which there were several times.

A few minutes ago was one of these times when she woke me by trying to step over my outstretched legs. She didn't manage to raise her first leg without kicking me and waking me from my 40 winks. It was after dawn at this time and we'd stopped at a town not far from my destination. I looked out the window at the passengers getting off. They didn't look too happy, but then tourists never do when they arrive at the bus terminal or airport arrivals. That's not what they've come to see. What took me away from the passengers' expressions was the expression and demeanour of someone else out there. My eyes fixated upon a man selling something that looked like sweet cornets. He had a dozen or so in a box which he placed on a stool acting as a display table. He moved the stool to intercept the flow of tourists wherever that flow headed. He began directly outside the door of the bus, then moved to stand next to those claiming their baggage from the storage of the bus. Finally he stood to the side of the bus where the tourists seemed to be dragging their bags to and then hauling them onto their backs.

It didn't look to be going well for him. Most people took a look at what he was offering and nothing more. In turn his shoulders seemed to drop and his face more disconsolate. I wondered if this was his only job, or if it was something extra to provide for his family. I wondered what his family was, how many kids did he have to put bread on the table for. How big was the roof over their heads?

I felt sorry for him and humbly remembered that there are many who have things a lot worse than me. Many people would be grateful to swap with me their problems for those I claim to have. The problems I have are of my own making and can be solved by my making too. That I must remember.

I was pleased to see him sell a few of his products to an elderly couple. But what could I actually do? Buy one of his things? Yes, I could. But what about the next guy selling something, shall I buy from him too? And the next? In towns like these everything revolves around the spending power of tourists. And when the tourists go home, the locals stay and must get by until the next tourist season. It's painful to watch people reliant on someone wanting or needing the product, or having to urge someone to buy it.

But again, what can I do? I'm not made of money, and am spending my savings on this trip. As do most backpackers. Sure, I have more than these people selling things but that doesn't mean I can or should buy from them. If I was rich then I'd buy all this man's things. And I'd pay for all the boat trips and horse rides and 4x4 drives offered to me. Even if I didn't want to go, I'd still pay the guide for the trip. I'd pay for them to go on the trip!

It's easy to say all this when you're not rich, that you'd help the poor. Doing it is another story and you should never forget where you come from.

I'm unlikely to ever make such exuberant amounts of money through my work so I'm reliant on either winning the lottery or marrying a rich girl. And out of those, I don't like the idea of being a gold-digger, plus winning the lottery seems much more likely.

Ah yes, the lottery, the answer to all my problems. If I won then I wouldn't need to work hard for anything. I could set up a café and a hostel without any need to compromise. And I could do it without working to save up the money or going to the bank for a loan. Plus if it didn't go well, I'd still have enough in reserve to continue my lifestyle. I wouldn't end up in a situation like this guy standing outside. Of course if only it were that easy. I think God knows that I want to win the lottery to solve my problems. Or that I'm relying on it. Because of that he won't let me win. He won't let me get what I want without working hard for it, earning it and eventually deserving it. Sometimes I think he sent Michaela to me to focus my mind on a plan for the future. Often she would ask me about a 2 or 3 year plan, about my career, about studying. When I told her about my wish to open my own café it led her to bug me about writing a business plan. 'Not now.' I used to tell her, 'In a few years' time.' Well now it's been a few years and God's still waiting. It's coming God, I promise. Just bear with me.

When I say that things would be better if I won the lottery, I mean that it would take away a lot of the distractions that working for a living brings. I mean when I'm at work I don't have the time to think about my ideal future. And after work I'm either too tired or I want to enjoy myself. If I could afford to stay at home then I'd think carefully and plan everything. Look at the Hollywood stars for example. They bleat on about doing this and that and how much yoga is good for their souls and exercise is for their bodies, but they're not out working from dawn until dusk to scrape enough money to put bread on the table. And when they do work they spend their time doing stupid things in front of a camera. When they get home, they don't need to clean the house, or make dinner, or go shopping, or help the kids with their homework. That could be me. If I had all that free time and didn't have to worry about making ends meet then obviously I'd change my lifestyle and give greater consideration to the world around me. Then I'd have the time to plan my café and hostel.

And a centre for homeless people. Food and shelter at no cost to them and no profit for me. I could afford it, so why would I need to make any money from them? And I'd regenerate poor underprivileged areas. Not like build a load of fancy flats and bars, but build everybody there a home, a school and some kind of cultural centre. Most of those people don't have an alternative to spending their time on crime and drugs. I'd try to help them, show them some of the other possibilities in the world. Aside from the money, I don't have the time to do such things, what with me having to work for my money. It makes me think that the rich should do more to help with such things. They've got plenty of money to start with and also lots of time, seeing as their ends are already met. If I had their money, I'd be making such an effort.

But God wants me to earn this status, that I should stand in the shoes of this man outside selling cornets instead of cutting corners. He's got a point. I'm sure this guy wouldn't refuse a lottery jackpot but I'm sure he's not relying on it either.

Chapter Thirty Seven

I stare at the ceiling through my flickering eyes. I'm about to fall asleep, of that I'm sure. I'm just waiting for it to happen. For so long I've resisted but now since my guard is down sleep doesn't come. I know it's only a matter of time. I'm too tired to stay awake.

Until then I stare at the ceiling and think of the day that will soon be.

This evening I arrived in the town of Villarrica in the Chilean Lake District. It's a nice small town with some German-influenced architecture and a pretty lake beside it. Dominating over the town is a 3000m active volcano with the same name as the town. I'd heard all about its gigantean presence but seeing it the first time for myself was very awe-inspiring. I was walking through the town, the buildings blocking the view, when the street opened up and there it was standing right ahead of me. The volcano's active so smoke is constantly blowing out of its crater and at night a red light is visible as the lava inside bubbles. It hasn't erupted since the 1970's which could mean it's due an eruption soon. Of course the people of Villarrica and the other surrounding towns wish for the next eruption to be delayed for as long as possible. To help with this superstitions and rituals are followed in order to keep the volcano happy and calm. Some of the superstitions I've heard about include never swearing when facing the volcano and no photos to be taken of it on the 1st and 15th days of each month. In the past an inhabitant of the town was picked out every second Sunday to take a basket of fruit and a bottle of rum to the volcano's summit. This was stopped a few years ago though for being silly.

Since I've been here I've regularly checked to see it's still in its placid state and that a river of lava isn't on its way to sweep me away. So far so good.

Before going to bed tonight I watched clouds gather around and hide it from view. Then the light darkened, leaving only the glowing red light up top. I then said to myself, 'I'll see you in the morning.' For tomorrow I'll ascend its 3000 metres and sit upon its peak.

Chapter Thirty Eight

It's morning now and trekking through the gaps in the clouds has taken me up most of the volcano. Around me I see blue sky and the volcano's summit within touching distance. The smoke blows from it high into the sky before disintegrating. The snow which has reflected the warm sun back at me for the last few hours is now taking on a darker and dirtier colour. I'm close now, very close to this volcano's beating heart.

Me and my tour group are taking one last break before going for the summit. We sit on the snow on an extreme angle of the volcano's face. I haven't sat on all of our breaks, mainly because I've been afraid of not getting up again. It's difficult for me to know where to put my feet and retain my balance when getting up. Doing it too fast could mean I slide down the mountain. Ok, I wouldn't fall all the way down and it wouldn't hurt but what an idiot I'd look. But then standing still hasn't been easy either. I've learned that I'm not very comfortable with not having my feet on a level surface, so standing with both feet on an angle whilst a couple of thousand metres high didn't feel so great. Plus there was the fear that I could fall back and take a tumble down. But this time I wanted to sit, my legs demanded it. It's been tough getting here.

Much like on that mountain the other day, I've been shown evidence that I'm not fit. And that I'm probably scared of heights too. But I'm here now and I'm not turning back. Aching legs are tiny problems to have and aren't going to stop me. I think about people who make trips like this out of necessity, transporting food and goods for their families, or children going to and from school. Here I am doing it for fun and complaining about it. The steepness, the snow, the heat, my small breakfast. Oh, poor you Doug. Get on with it you wimp. There are always bigger problems and people in worse situations. Don't forget that. And also, those people's problems aren't usually of they're own making. I chose to go for this summit; no one stuck a gun to my head. If I don't like the way it's going, that's my own fault. And if I want to abandon the idea and walk back down, then do it. It'll be my decision too. No guns at anyone's head. But then if tomorrow I'm angry for bottling out and regret my decisions, then it's me who's to blame. No one else Doug, just you.

It's been partly down to diatribes like this that I have got this far. To distract me from my fear and fatigue my mind has thought of all kinds of things. I've sung different songs in my head, recited scenes from films, made a list of people to email, thought again about what to do when I get home to England. It's all helped. It's all put me in a focused state and the only times I've slipped out of it is when we've stopped for a rest, like now.

But now we're getting up again. I put my backpack on again, which isn't so easy as doing it too quickly could tip my balance and send me rolling down like a bowling ball headed for the trekker pins below. This time there's no problem and I plant my right foot into an already made print and get myself near the front of our trekking herd. I'm in a group of about 8 lads doing this trek. The others all know each other. They're from Israel and have just finished their military service. When I heard this at the beginning it concerned me that they would be used to such exercise and that their superior strength and speed would leave me trailing. Fortunately that hasn't been the case. About four of them have been bringing up the rear since the start and been complaining about it too. The others and myself have been up ahead with the leader setting the pace and then waiting for them when it's been rest time. I remember how tired I felt when we started but that's given way during the trek to a greater feeling of strength and mental calm. That's partly down to my fellow trekkers. I can't be that bad if they're lagging so far behind and sound like they're going to die. Plus, the embarrassing thought of giving up and walking back down alone has driven me to keep going. And now here I am, almost at the end.

I walk with my head down and my eyes fixed on the footprint in front. Left foot, right foot. Keep your balance. Don't lean to the left, nor the right, dead centre. Ignore what's to the side; it's just a flat field of white snow. Not a vast open land spread out below you. What's happened to my distractions? Why can't I think of something to occupy my mind? It's only a matter of time before I begin to think about earthquakes again. What if one hit me now? This volcano would open up and its boiling blood would come bursting out and sweep me down to the bottom. There are guided treks up here every day so I suppose at some point a group would get hit by an eruption. Knowing my luck it'll be now just as I'm reaching the top. I wonder if I'd get a refund.

Our path has begun to straighten out and I can see people sitting up ahead. Is this the end? I hadn't really imagined what the summit would look like. From the bottom it looked like a small point with smoke bellowing out. From up here it's a giant black hole with smoke bellowing out. There's room to sit around the crater and it's here our guide tells us to rest and take in the views.

I sit on brown and black sand and see small yellow rocks around me. It feels like a psychedelic beach. Behind me is the giant hole from where the growling sound of the lava is coming from. I get as close to the edge as possible to look down in the hope of seeing some lava. But I only manage to see darkness brightened by the rising smoke.

I turn around to look at the view from the volcano instead. I no longer feel afraid or apprehensive about being up here. Maybe it's because of the thrill of making it, of succeeding. I sit here now in peace, relaxed. Ahead of me I see a blue din made up of sky, mountains and other volcanoes. Whereas upon that mountain a few days ago I had a sheet of cloud blocking my view of the world below, today I only have a few small clouds dotted around obscuring my view of a lake and one of the small towns in the region. I can vaguely see a car driving on a road through a field. Only because I'm already looking at that point and the car is moving, otherwise I wouldn't know it was there. Yesterday when looking at the volcano I tried to look for people climbing it. I squinted my eyes and used the zoom on my camera but couldn't see anyone. I wonder now if anyone can see me up here. Judging by the bright yellow Ghostbusters outfit I've been made to wear, everyone should be able to see me. In fact geologists are probably concerned at the bright yellow thing upon their volcano.

Chapter Thirty Nine

I'm woken by sounds and noises outside my window. Are they sounds or are they noises? They say noise is unwanted sound. I don't like what I'm hearing and wish for it to go away so I suppose you'd call that unwanted sound. The most prominent noise I can hear is that of the rain dropping against the window. Drop, drop, drop, drop! Like someone's tapping their fingers against it. The window's only made of thin glass so each wave of raindrops rattles it and sounds and feels like it's going to smash through the glass. And there's the wind too, shaking the window – its frame, making vibrations all across the wall beside which lies my bed.

I've had a very interrupted night's sleep, worse than the other night when everyone's shouting woke me up. That time it was just the morning that was disturbed; I think it's been raining almost all night this time. I remember waking at one point without the noise of rain. But I could hear cars driving through puddles and people walking on wet gravel outside. I managed to get back to sleep then though, something I don't think I will be doing this time. I lie on my back and stare at the ceiling, eyes firmly open and mind as alert as it can be under the circumstances.

Lying still like this gives me a strange sensation. Subconsciously, I think, my body is swaying left and right, like the day after being on a boat. This has to be down to how I got back down the volcano yesterday. From the summit each of us sat on a small plastic sledge, like a tea tray, and slid down like we were kids and school had been closed for the day because of snow. We didn't descend the full 3000m in one go, that'd probably be too much, but slid a few hundred metres in different goes.

It was great, something I'd love to do again. For me as someone who's only had one useless attempt at skiing, this was a consolation and a decent substitute. I travelled as quickly as I could, aware of the dangers, but also aware of the thrills. It was a fantastic use of the adrenaline surging through my veins after reaching the volcano's summit and a great way to round off the day.

Sadly at the moment it feels like I've come crashing back down with a bump. I can still hear rain outside and the window shaking. I get up to take a look outside and see if it's as bad as I fear. It's not. It's just gloomy. I've been spoilt the last few weeks with hot sunny weather almost all day, everyday.

I look over to where the volcano usually stands over the town. It's not there, it can't be seen. The clouds are so thick that they're blocking view of the volcano. And they're so low that not even the bottom of it is visible.

Or maybe it was never there.

No, it's there. It's just covered by the clouds. Either that or it's hiding from me, cowering and bowing its head because I reached its peak and got huge satisfaction from it. I came, I saw and I conquered. And now I can't see it.

Alright, time to start the day. Let's get dressed and have that all important coffee. There's no point letting the weather get me down, I can't do anything about that. And as for the lack of sleep, I can make that up on my journey today; it's going to be a long one. I'm going home.

Chapter Forty

The long journey ahead of me begins here in Villarrica. I'm taking the bus back to Santiago and from there will fly to London.

I find my seat on the bus and immediately push it back so I can recline and stretch my legs. It's still raining as we leave Villarrica and head for the countryside. This region of Chile is known as the Lake District due to its numerous lakes. But it's also part of the lush green Chilean south. Here all fertile land is full of grass and plants, large green trees stand tall and close together, hills rise and fall far into the distance, homes have flowers in their gardens. Now the grey sky doesn't seem so dull. In fact it's a wonderful contrast to the colourful palette underneath it. In many ways it reminds me of England. Especially in that it was scenes like these that I saw on the day I left England to come here. All that time ago it feels like now.

Sitting back, watching the world pass by without a concern is very relaxing and I don't think it'll be long until I start catching up on my lack of sleep. But then my attention is diverted away from the window to a tall dark shadow in the aisle beside my seat. I turn to see what it is.

"Hello. I thought it was you."

It's the man I met on the bus before.

"Nice to see you again."

He doesn't wait for an invitation before sitting himself down beside me.

"You're travelling back to Santiago?"

"Yes, I am. And then flying home to London."

"Oh, so this is the end of your trip?"

I nod.

"How has it been? Have you enjoyed yourself?"

"Yes, I've had a great time. I've visited some lovely places and met some interesting people. It's a shame to be leaving."

"Ah, but you know, it's important to take your holiday spirit home with you. I can never understand when people get depressed when returning home after a holiday. They should be refreshed and have a different outlook or perspective on things."

He keeps his eyes fixed on me.

"Do you not think so?"

"Yes. It's easy to say that when you're lying on the beach with all the time in the world. But it can be difficult to maintain once the routines of everyday life kick in again."

He takes in my point, nodding his head.

"In a perfect world people would have the holiday spirit all the time."

"No, don't tell me this about a perfect world!"

He turns his head away and raises his arm in disgust.

"People say, 'in a perfect world I'd do this and the world would be like that'. What's stopping people from realising that? What big obstacles are blocking people from making changes to their lives that will improve them and make them happier?"

I look at the back of the seat in front of me. This conversation's got a little deeper than I'd hoped it would. I look back at the man, him expecting me to say something.

"Erm…" That's all I have to say.

He turns back to me, staring into my eyes again.

"Tell me, when you get home will you wear a smile on your face and be nice to people like you've done whilst you've been here?"

"Erm, yeah, I'll try."

"See, that's not so difficult, is it?"

He looks at me like he's telling me the simplest logic in the world. And I suppose he's right. Why can't I be as happy at home as I have been here? And if things get bad I can always recall my time here and the memories that made me so happy.

His face then turns into a small smirk as he asks me, "Or will you get bogged down with the problems you had before coming here? People asking you for money in the street, offering you drugs on the bus, car drivers hurrying you across the street as you cross, bus drivers not stopping for you."

I give him a bemused look. Does he know those things happened to me or does he just think they're general problems for everyone?

"Or fighting boys outside pubs and leaving their girlfriends in tears on the pavement. Need I go on?"

"How do you…"

"It's not important how I happen to know these things. What's important is that…"

"I think it is important that you tell me…"

"No, it's not really."

And with that I'm silenced. There's something about his look that makes me want to say nothing, to only listen. He stares at me in silence for a few seconds, holding it until he's sure I won't interrupt him again.

199

"It's really not important how I know these things, that you must realise. That's only a small detail. There are some things in life which are important and should be treated as such. The rest is just mess, clutter, background stuff."

He relents his stare, his eyes no longer solely fixed on mine.

"It's up to the individual to clear through this and find the important stuff. For some it's difficult to distinguish the two. For some the answer is different. You Doug have been spending too much time and energy on trivial matters."

I feel the hold over me loosen and the need to speak return.

"But if it's up to the individual to find what's important, shouldn't you be leaving me to it?"

He smiles at my question. I can't decipher what that means.

"And if the answer is different for different people, why are you trying to influence my thinking?"

"You're tougher than I'd initially supposed. I didn't think you would be brave enough to ask so many questions."

Why would I need to be brave? Should I be scared of something? This man's just strange more than scary. He keeps smiling as he stares at me again.

"Don't you ever feel that you're being tested? That something's being put in your path to test how you cope and overcome it? They appear in many different forms and can be difficult to recognise. People say they want this and they want to be like that, yet when they're confronted by a test where they can prove themselves, they more often than not fail, usually blaming somebody else's interference or what they deem to call bad luck or fate."

"I feel that yours is a life that needs intervening. You've been on a slippery slope for a while, haven't you? Making problems for yourself. Not knowing how to deal with them. I thought you could do with a helping hand."

"Who are you? How do you know so much about me?"

"You are a brave young soul, aren't you? Not many usually have the required ingredients to ask me such questions." he smirks, not at all disguising his mocking tone. "Maybe you're strong enough after all."

"Strong enough for what?"

'Strong enough for what?' I hear him whisper to himself.

"I've been keeping an eye on you for some time, monitoring you, shall we say?"

"Aha, we met on the bus before and I also saw you on the sand dunes."

"Did you?" he laughs. "And there was me thinking I'd found such a good hiding place."

He continues laughing to himself. I'm not sure he's aware he's doing it.

"And the other times, did you see me then?"

What other times?

"There have been other times you should have seen me. I've been watching you while you've been here."

He's not good at hiding his mock surprise. He's playing with me. Though it does help that he knows what this is all about.

"Tell me, do you remember your dreams?"

"Not always."

"Ah, that's probably why you haven't seen me so much."

He then sits in silence for a minute or so. He turns his gaze to the opposite window, looking away from me.

"I can see you're surprised and don't really understand. I'll give you a moment to think about this."

That's nice of him.

"You haven't been doing so great over the last few months, have you? You've needed a helping hand but been afraid to ask for it. But you've done so much better since you've been here. I can see your perspective is changing, your priorities are different. Your strength is greater."

"This must continue once you arrive home. Don't let yourself get sucked into the same rut as before. We don't want another near-death experience, do we?"

"Hmmm? Yes, I know about that too."

"I thought that by having death stare at you, it'd make you realise what's important to you in life."

He stares at me as he says this. Holding the stare, not moving his eyes at all. I know he means me and those pills but could he mean something else? Is there something he's not telling me?

"Are you Death? Is that why you've been watching me?"

"No." he laughs.

"Are you God?"

"No, I'm not God either."

"You seem God-like. You seem to have all the answers."

He smiles, like he's trying to appear humble,

"I don't have all the answers, I just guide people towards them. I'm a very experienced man."

He's not God, he's not Death. He's an experienced man. Or a crazy man. Why do they always sit next to me?"

"Tell me, would you behave differently if you knew you were going to die soon?"

"Yes, probably."

"And what would you do?"

Off the top of my head I can't think of anything, my mind's blank. There's lots I'd do, that I've already thought about. I just can't remember right now.

"Many things."

"Ok, you don't have to tell me. But why don't you do these things now? Why doesn't anyone? Everyone's lives are going to end soon, that's a fact. Don't wait until the last second, do it now! What's stopping you? Hmm?"

He's right about that. What is stopping me? Everything I want to be, I want to do, I want to accomplish is within me. I need to grab it and release it. I can at least try, otherwise what's the point of my life?

He looks out of the window again, gazing at the passing fields and trees.

"Everyone leaves a mark on the world and is remembered in some way. Remembered by those close to you, your friends and family. The mark left by some is bigger than others, it's remembered by the outside world, you might call it. Don't worry or feel jealous about this. These people just have better PR. It doesn't mean the marks they've left are better or bigger than yours."

He turns back to me, looking less intense than before, now a little more solemn, I suppose.

"What's your mark going to be? How are people going to remember you?"

I look out of the window at the lush colours whizzing past us.

"Because once you're dead you don't have any more say in the matter."

I look back and see that he's gone, disappeared. Back from where he came I can only suppose.

Chapter Forty One

I feel strangely excited. Not because I'm leaving and I've had an awful time but because I've had a great time and I want to get home to tell people about it. I want to share my experiences and memories. Also, I'm excited and somewhat eager to take home my new sense of spirit, the new confidence I've found whilst here. My grip on the direction of where my life is heading. I want to prove to myself that it's not just a temporary thing because I'm on holiday. This is for good. This is the first day of the rest of my life.

I've taken to heart what that man told me on the bus. It seemed to make a fair amount of sense. I have to make my life worthwhile, starting from now. I don't know when it'll end so I should make the most of it.

The question of who that man was is another matter altogether. I've never encountered anything like that before and I wonder if I will again. Will he return to talk to me again? Is he still checking on me now? He said he was 'guiding me to the answers.' He seemed to do ok actually. I do feel at least closer to the answer of what I'm going to do about my life. It's stuck with me what he said about leaving a mark on people to remember you by. I don't think people often see how or what you really are, or what you intend. You have to show them this, show them proof of what you are. At the end of it all, they'll be the ones writing my obituary. And I want to make sure I approve of it.

I didn't manage to get any sleep on the bus in the end. After the man left my mind was too busy ticking over to then switch off and let me sleep. But now I'm on the plane bound for London and I'm more hopeful. That is if the passenger in the seat beside me will stop fidgeting. In constant two second intervals he readjusts his position in his seat, looks around at what's happening on the plane and then rustles his newspaper. For what? I don't know. I'm trying not to let it bother me, for as I'm learning, I should only let important things bother me. But it's very annoying for me in the tired state I'm currently in. Even as I'm drifting off I can still feel him twitching.

"It makes you wonder what awaits us back home, doesn't it?" I hear a voice say, seemingly from the seat next to me.

I open my eyes and there is indeed my fellow passenger looking at me, expecting a response.

"Eh? All this trouble back home, makes you wonder if we're heading back to a warzone, doesn't it?"

Trouble back home? Warzone? That was nothing I knew about. Are we being invaded?

"What do you mean?" the politest response I could think of, though not the most accurate of describing my feelings at this exact time.

"All this." he says and smacks the page of the newspaper resting on his left leg. I suppose he means a story in the paper. I've hardly read the news at all while

I've been away and have no idea what kind of trouble could be going on.

"What's going on? I haven't been following the news."

"All these protesters in London," he says, smacking the paper again, "barricading the streets. Not happy with the government."

"Oh."

"Been fighting with riot police the last few days." now shaking his head. I guess he's against the protests.

"I don't know. Some people just don't know how to behave nowadays."

Do I let this go or do I speak up? I don't want to get into a heavy discussion but I don't want to keep hiding my opinion either.

"But people are allowed to protest, you know?"

"Of course, but they shouldn't go around starting fights and trashing places. These are just hooligans."

"Maybe the police got violent first."

"No. No way." vehemently shaking his head. "Not our police. They don't ever throw the first punch. They don't even carry guns."

I wonder if he's going to tell me that they work for nothing but the honour of Queen and country and that they eat jam scones for lunch.

"No, these hoodlums don't care what they're protesting about."

"What are they protesting about?"

"I don't know. They're not happy with something the government's done or hasn't done. Just making a nuisance from what I can see."

"So shouldn't they protest if they're not happy? It's better and more useful than sitting around moaning about it."

"Hmmm…"

He doesn't seem convinced. He looks at me like I'm from a different planet. I feel like if this was the 50's during the McCarthy witch hunts he'd be reporting me.

In my view it's good to protest about something you're not happy about instead of just moaning and complaining about it. This way the government, or whoever, knows you're not happy. Maybe nothing will come of it but at least something's trying to be done, instead of just being talked about. But there are different ways of protesting and one involving violence is not one I agree with. If you want to cause trouble then you are a hooligan like this man says.

"As for the violence, we don't know if the ones fighting went there to protest in the first place or to cause violence."

"No, I…" he splutters, his face frowning, still looking suspicious of me and my opinion. "Oh, look…" he says, turning away towards the front of the plane, "the film's coming on."

I turn too and see the giant screen at the front of the plane switch on. The man to my right seems engrossed in it, his face lighting up like a child's. I guess this signals the end of our conversation. It's one of those films about a man and a woman who start of not liking each other but then do and finally fall in love. For me, sleep seems like a better option. Maybe watching the first few minutes of this will close my eyes.

It doesn't work immediately so I instead glance back over to this man's newspaper, still spread open upon his lap. Since I last looked at it he's turned the page and now I can see a headline proclaiming that unemployment is down. That's good I suppose, something those protesters can't complain about. If people are working then they'll have money in their pocket and that's always a good thing, isn't it?
I wonder though how many of those are employed in unnecessary jobs, like the paparazzi for example. Is it necessary to take photos of famous people everyday? When the famous people are working, then fine, I understand. But why when they're out shopping or eating lunch? Maybe it's just me but I don't understand.

And I don't understand either why people working for newspapers or magazines buy the photos to print. And then there are magazines devoted solely to such photos and the gossip surrounding them. But then it keeps people employed I suppose, and unemployment rates down.

I think of paparazzi once more as I look over to the next page of the paper. There are photos of that woman who sings and is on that show every week wearing a new outfit. She's in the papers a lot too. Everyday there seems to be a story about her, about what she's done, what she's going to do, what she's said. It's another thing I wonder how necessary it is to us. Do we need to know everything about her? I know I could survive without it. But again, people are being employed and paid to write about her. And without these stories what would be left of the newspaper? Stories about politics and crime probably. Journalists wouldn't have jobs without bad news, well at the same time they wouldn't have jobs without people like her.

At least the stories about her life distract us from the harsher aspects of our world. So that's a good thing to come out of it I suppose. We can't concern ourselves with war and corruption and economics and the environment if we only get to know about the news surrounding people like her.

I wonder if that's her intention. Does she let the country read all about her life so we have something to distract us and possibly cheer ourselves up? Or does she have any say in the matter at all? Does she ask that her life goes out in print or is it all the work of a PR person? A PR guru, I think they're called.

Still, it all means more people are on the payroll and fewer are on the dole claiming benefits. Maybe some of those could get such jobs.

Chapter Forty Two

My mind won't switch off. For what now seems like hours I've laid here trying to sleep, without success. Tilting my neck back I can see behind the curtain and out of the window. The night sky is a dark purple blotted with damp grey clouds. In the glare of the light from the lamppost snow falls.

It's snowed for days since I returned. The roads and pavements are full of snow and ice. Most cars are snowed in and owners are leaving them where they are. Those able to move find themselves sliding uncontrollably along roads, or down hills if like the street where I live. The street next to mine is also on a hill so going out at all at the moment is quite a test of balance, patience and ice skating ability. Of course it'd be a whole lot easier if the local council organised some grit to be laid down. But that hasn't happened for whatever reason. Maybe the person responsible doesn't realise it's snowing. I understand that these things can be difficult but I'll try to remember this the next time the council tax is raised. You know, that tax that pays for grit, not such luxuries as men outside with pickaxes and shovels. Not the tax that pays for the bruises old people get when they fall over on the icy pavement, or the missed day at work for the man who can't drive his car up the frozen hill.

Maybe I won't pay the bill next time. I'll be taken to court for not paying my money as I should. What will happen to the council for not spending it as they should?

I want to get to sleep. I feel I've got lots of energy to burn and inspiration to tap into. I've been back home for a few days now and it feels like now I should start to take some action regarding my life. I spent the first few days relaxing, settling back in, meeting friends and family, telling them about my trip. But now the fun of that is wearing off and I feel boredom and/or lethargy could be just around the corner.

As expected, I've returned home with very little money. And the pleasant surprise that awaited my return home means that I'll have even less this month. Among the junk mail packed into my post box was a polite letter informing me that I shall now be obliged to pay more money in order to keep my current roof over my head. There was nothing stated whether the two mice who share the flat with me will also be exposed to the increase. I can't complain too much because I imagine the extra money from the tenants will pay for the repair of the squeaky floorboards, the secure windows we were told we'd be getting and/or a higher wage for the girl who comes to clean the building every Tuesday between 9 and 10.

Fortunately I got a new job two days after returning home. Unfortunately my increase in rent doesn't correspond to an increase in salary. I'll be earning about £6 an hour for cleaning the offices and workstations of a bank's HQ. I don't mean to be ungrateful, I should be very grateful for the privilege, those bankers employed there could quite easily polish their own computer screens, wipe hummus off their keyboards and put cans of coke into their bins – yet they leave it for me, and they pay me for it.

I'm just thankful to have a job and some money coming in again – my trip left me more than a little dry. Though my plans for setting up a café or a hostel will have to wait a little longer whilst I save some money. Once I've deducted rent, bills, food and transport from my wages, I should be able to start putting together a little nest egg and something to show the bank manager when he asks how much I'll be paying towards the venture.

From next door I can hear the sound of the radio, one of those talk-only stations. All day they've been discussing the protests that are still going on, probably are now too at this hour. The station's even got its advertising promos based around them. Why not use a bloody aggressive protest to promote your station's 24 hour broadcasting coverage live and in HD, on digital, online and on demand.

I don't know how many days it's been now but the protesters don't seem to be ready to back down or give up. Following the news since my return I feel there's a lot to protest about. It seems there are cuts to public funding all over the place – most significantly in hospitals, schools, libraries and the police- the most fundamental institutions in this country. Small businesses are folding up and people are losing their jobs. People up and down this country are now seeing their plans and hopes for their lives become ruined and it's the fault of the bankers and the politicians who let them get away with it. The people feel powerless. Why shouldn't they express their anger?

But then what good are these protests producing? The protesters and police are clashing and people like the one I met on the plane believe this is the sole purpose of the protesters. Any sympathy or understanding for their cause is being lost because of these riots. I can imagine the government's happy for this to continue as it keeps the focus off of them and their failing of the people. It might concern them that people are getting hurt each day and the city's getting damaged but often this needs to happen for a government to get through dark moments. Not that I'm suggesting they've encouraged this violence.

Is there much point to these protests? Will the government end its cuts policy because people aren't happy? Is anything going to change because of this? I think this is a storm the government just wants to ride out. Soon the media will concentrate on something else and will stop recounting the problems and the views of these people hurt by the cuts and the government will have got away with it. 'Life goes on, no one's angry any more, what shall we do next?'

The bankers and politicians are taking care of themselves but who's taking care of us?
Was it their intention when they began their careers, 'stuff those we're supposed to be serving!'? Or was it to

help people? Perhaps they should be reminded why they wanted this job in the first place. It doesn't matter which wing they belong to, what matters is that they do an honest job and protect the welfare of the people who give them the power.

Should I do anything about it? Is it something I should be concerning myself with? Things will never change if nothing's done. There must be something I can do. I'm annoyed by the dishonesty and cheating of these politicians and the unfairness dealt out to the people who put them there. It annoys me much like the behaviour of people did before I went away. Behaviour which seems quite irrelevant now. Just like the man on the bus in Chile told me, that 'There are some things in life which are important and should be treated as such.' Maybe this is such a thing. Maybe I can try to do something about this. It's about time I stopped moaning about things and did something about them. Something beneficial for other people, not just myself. Something worth putting my energy into.

Chapter Forty Three

My new job's not that bad after all. I'm able to go about it without being supervised or scrutinised by someone, I can listen to music in my earphones or just let my mind wander and concentrate on something more interesting. Tonight I'm working the night shift, as I have done the last few nights after putting in a request. I've used those previous nights to perform acts which will culminate tonight.

As I make my way around the desks on the 9th floor I leave a note on each computer screen. The note contains facts and figures relating to the crisis caused by some of the people who work in this building; the cuts in public service budgets, the bonuses of the bankers, the businesses that have gone bust, the people who can't afford their homes, the bankers who have bought new sports cars, the tax avoided by certain companies. At the bottom of the note is a small statement that reads, 'Why was it you wanted this job? To help or destroy people? You've destroyed them, now's the time to help them.'

This is the final piece of the work I've been doing here the last few nights. I imagine it's going to be my last night of employment in this bank as one look at the security videos will reveal who it was who stuck these notes to the screens and I'll be asked to leave. Previously this week I've had short friendly chats with the managers who've been burning the midnight oil, working hard at their desks while I've cleaned around them. Over there in that office in the corner I see the person who I'm going to have tonight's chat with.

I enter through the office door. He doesn't look away from his computer screen, I don't know if he saw me come in, and acknowledging me would probably be too much to ask for. I carry a cloth and a pot of spray in case even though in this office I have no intention of cleaning anything, they're just a guise. I step around the back of him. He looks at a screen containing charts of numbers. At least he seems to be doing some work and not looking at Facebook or some other website.

I softly put my hands on his shoulders. I don't want to be aggressive, what I'm doing is intended to be done peacefully and calmly, without bloodshed and violence.

"Don't worry, I'm not going to hurt you." I tell him, my mouth next to his right ear. I then grab a firmer hold on his shoulders. Again, not because I want to hurt him, but just to keep him in his place. I don't want him leaving before he hears what I have to say.

"You and your friends have created one or two problems for everyone, haven't you? How does it go? 'Never before has so much been owed by so few to so many.'? I'm not good with quotes."

I can feel his body shake and see sweat on his shirt as it gathers in between his shoulder blades. I still keep a firm grip of him.

"I'm not going to hurt you. I just want you to listen to me." I look at his face. He seems to understand

218

enough. I ask him to be certain. "Do you understand?" He nods his head.

"Now, because of the game of roulette you and your mates played, and lost, many people can't afford enough food to eat, a roof to live under, a car to drive or a university education. That's without mentioning all the things you can afford, your possessions for example. What car do you drive, by the way?"

"A Ferrari."

"Why? Why not something more modest?"

"Because I can afford it." He hesitates to say, realising perhaps that it's not the answer he wants to give.

"Yes, because you can afford it. Many people could never afford it, now they can barely afford to take the bus. How does that make you feel? Maybe sad, guilty, responsible?" I look at his face for his reaction. He shakes his head. "Or happy maybe?"

"No, of course not!" he suddenly jolts and tries to turn around to face me. My grip doesn't change though and he stays where he is. After resisting, he takes a deep sigh and bows his head. "It wasn't my entire fault. Why are you picking on me?"

I'm not just picking on him. I've done this to three other guys earlier in the week. But I don't want him to know that.

"Who should I be picking on?" I nudge the back of his seat with my knee. "Huh? Who?!"

"All the managers and supervisors, they all knew what was going on and what was going to happen."

"Aha, and you know who these people are?"

"Yes, yes, I can give you their names. And their pictures if you like."

"No, no, that's not necessary." I don't need to know any other names having already paid visits to colleagues of this one. "I wish for you to do something else for me."

"Yes, yes. What is it?" he says excitedly, eager to please. His body getting sweatier.

"What I want is for you to give a little back of what you've gained from this."

"What do you mean?"

"I know a lot rests on your shoulders, if the economy is strong it means you've worked hard and you therefore should be well rewarded. But when the economy's on the floor, like it is now, it means you perhaps haven't worked as well and therefore shouldn't be so well rewarded, like you are now. Don't get me wrong, I'm not saying you shouldn't get paid. You have to for the work you've done. But the bonuses you receive, they're a little excessive, don't you think? Why do you need a bonus on top of your comfy salary when the work you've done doesn't merit it? If I don't clean this office, I lose my job. I don't get given more money from the public to try and do a better job the next time. I'm no economics expert, I have to listen to what you lot tell me and trust you."

"Now, what do I want you to do about it?"

"What I want for you to do is pay an amount of money, determined by yourself, into the accounts of each person who has an account with this bank. You will also regularly donate a sum of money to charities, hospitals, libraries and schools."

I intently watch his face as I tell him this. A look comes over him. I guess you'd call it bewilderment, or amazement. Or maybe fear even. I have no special desire as to how he should feel. And I'm not going to ask him.

"Think of yourself as Robin Hood. A dizzy Robin perhaps. You took from the poor and gave to the rich and now you'll give back to the poor."

I imagine his mind's wondering about his own fortune dwindling through his coming acts of charity. In any case I give him a little tip.

"If you find yourself getting a little short, you can always sell the Ferrari, can't you? Most people survive without one, don't they? Don't worry, a bus or train will get you around too."

Now I lift his face up so it looks up at mine and give his shoulders a little shake.

221

"Hmm? How does that sound? The country will be back on its feet in no time."

"Uh, huh, ok." he appears unsure or unconvinced. I let his head sit where it should. "Is there anything else?"

"No. That's all for now. I'll be back if there's more I'd like you to do." I relax my grip on his shoulders. My hands feeling very moist. "Don't make me come back to check back on you."

I spin his chair around and we look face to face.

"And that's it. You can relax."

"You're not going to hurt me?"

"No, why would I hurt you? Your bruises would heal in a few days and we'd be back to where we were. Unless I kill you…" His mouth drops and his eyes widen. "…which I won't."

I stand up straight and take a step back.

"I'm free to go?"

"No, I'm free to go. You stay here, you have work to do." I give him a look which intends to tell him that the work I've set him to do begins immediately and must not be compromised. Of course that's partly dependant on one thing he needs to be told.

I head towards the door out of his office. "In return for me not hurting you, you will tell no one about me coming here tonight. Not your wife, your colleagues, and not the police. Understand?" He nods. As do I. "Good."

I turn the handle on the door and open it. Before stepping through I look back, "Anyway, what could you tell them I've done? Since when has appealing to someone's conscience, heart and soul been a crime?"

Chapter Forty Four

The noise continuously fills my head and surrounds my personal space. I sit as far away from the epicentre as possible, though still keeping myself in sight, ready for my turn to be called. Sitting at the end of the reception area furthest from me is the woman who will eventually give me the signal to enter. It appears best that I wait by watching her as I won't hear her in this noise. Her two telephones ring endlessly. When she puts down the receiver it only manages to restart the ringing, as if it's the only thing they do. What she's saying is a mystery. From this position she looks to be miming to the infinite number of people calling.

Sitting in the two seats closest to her are two people arguing, a young girl and an older man. From where I sit I can't pinpoint the reason for their argument, I can only hear some ambiguous adjectives like star quality, A-list and fashion icon. The young girl's trying to hold back tears it seems. I think she said something about 'only ever wanting to sing.' To which I almost definitely heard the man reply, 'You can sing as much as you like but no one will ever hear any of it without these peoples' help. Nothing comes for free, you know that.' Their murmuring, though mildly less annoying than the ringing phones, only adds to the cacophony of noise in this enclosed room.

Pacing up and down in front of me is a man with a mobile phone seemingly stuck to the left side of his head. Each time he approaches me it's audibly clear to me what he yells down the mouthpiece, "If he doesn't give us the front page, we'll go somewhere else." is followed by "We've spent too much money on this tart to let it get pushed back to where people stop noticing."

Only when he sees me looking at him does he hide his mouth with his hand, though that's mostly because he wants to keep quiet what he's saying rather than how he's saying it.

Out of the corner of my eye I see the woman at the reception desk wave her left hand above her head. I look up and see her balancing two phones on either side of her neck, writing something with her right hand whilst waving at me with the left. Her face creases and points to the door in the corner. I take this as my cue to enter.

As I make my way across the long room I get a look at the pictures that hang on the wall in front of which I was just sitting. Each one is a framed copy of a front page of this best selling newspaper. One after the other, their giant black and white headlines bark their opinion of the news at you, joined by a photo in case you don't understand puns. Editions from more recent years contain coupons for discounted holidays and computers for schools. My old Nan used to say they were the only reason she bought the paper, along with the TV guide and horoscopes. And for the chip shop she used to run. Otherwise she wasn't interested.

I approach the door and realise I have no expectations of what awaits me on the other side. I've never seen a newspaper editor before. I've no idea what one looks like or how they behave. All I've ever known of them previously is from what they've chosen to show me through their medium of communication.

I open the door and see something like the male equivalent of the woman I've just left on the reception. His free hand waves me inside and gestures to me to sit down in front of his desk, while the fingers of the other hand tap impatiently at the phone they're gripping. Much like the man on the mobile outside he seems to put his point of view across in an aggressive manner. I wonder if this is his only manner.

He abruptly ends the conversation and puts down the phone before sighing deeply and giving me a look that seems to imply that I should share his empathy for the person on the other end. He lifts himself from his seat and puts his right arm out across his desk.

"I'm Daniel Simpson, the editor." he tells me. I shake his outstretched hand and accept his invitation to sit down. He sits too, up close to his desk, his elbows resting on it. "I hear you have an interesting story to offer us."

He immediately wants to discuss business. Again, I didn't know what to expect, small-talk, chit-chat.

"Yeah, I…"

"I have to warn you, we have some big ones in the queue ahead of you. You saw them waiting outside? The juice they have is going to take some beating."

I'm confident the story I have to propose is more important and more relevant than what they have to offer.

"I…"

But if I can't let it be known.

"You have means of entrapping of a celeb into admitting his crimes and misdemeanours, I gather."

"Yeah, that's righ…"

"Alright, but we have people whose role is to do this day in and day out. We're not against having someone from outside helping out, after all, some public knowledge needs help being disclosed." He brings his chair even closer to the desk. "Whether we accept the story, where we eventually print it – front page, showbiz column, mystery guess-who column – depends on the size of the story and the size of the celeb." He rubs his fingers and thumb together. "And how much money it'd cost to get the story."

He licks his lips and his eyes stare expectantly at mine.

"Now's when you tell me who it is."

"It's actually a politician, not a celeb."

"Ok… But you've got him admitting to a scandal, yeah? What is it? Drugs, women, money laundering?"

His face goes from a pleased smirk to something more curious. He licks his lips like a predator seeing meat in front of its eyes.

"Not exactly."

"Then what exactly?!"

He grows anxious as he realises this meat won't be served to him on a plate.

"I have access to a politician who will admit to and apologise for all his abuse of power and privilege, his misuse of the public's trust."

He clasps his hands together and holds them in front of his mouth. He then takes in a large breath before breathing out deeply and turning his focus towards me.

"And then what? What would you want us to do?"

"Print it on your front pages. Set up a crusade. Scare them all. If they know you're against them, they'll believe the public is too, won't they? Don't they always believe the papers' opinions equal the public's?"

His mouth stretches to a knowing smile. To knowing what, I'm not sure exactly. Maybe it pleases him to hear from someone else that politicians fear his printed words. The smile is then joined by a frown. The two of them competing for supremacy. Eventually the smile gives way.

"But we do those crusades, campaigns, tirades, whatever, for a reason. It needs a goal. It has to bring about a change." I can see imaginary thought bubbles filled with question marks bursting above his head. He looks straight-faced directly at me, "Why are you doing this? What do you want from it?" He looks away, imagining a possible answer. "A change in political system?"

"There aren't many different political systems around. What I'd like is more honesty and truth from those who are a part of it. Do the job they're supposed to."

He slowly nods his head in agreement.

"That's a good thing to want, but I'd be out of a job for a start."

He smiles. It pleases me he has a sense of humour. Maybe he doesn't in fact take his work so seriously.

But then that frown returns.

He looks over to the pile of papers sitting beside him on his desk. Maybe he feels able to take care of other business whilst speaking to me. The conversation no longer merits him speaking to me face to face.

"It won't change anything. Everyone knows they abuse their power, they always have done. People are used to it, they expect it. It'll all blow over. Commissions and inquiries will be set up and, if they're not fiddled, will come up with very little. Just something to appease you. Then it'll blow over. That's what happens. That's what's happened with everything we've ever done. The man you have in mind will probably resign, but what does it matter if it's just one guy?"

I can't let it blow over. It'll blow over and nothing will change if everyone says it won't or can't. If everybody did something, anything, to make it change, then it very possibly might. At least it'd be a step forward. Instead a man here, who has means of access to the public and those in power, appears to let it be. A man, who could be part of the solution, is a big part of the problem.

"That's why we should go after all of them. Print headlines of them everyday, of what they've done and not done. And ask them why. Get to the heart of it, not just some lines an aide has scribbled down to fend you off. They're elected by us to govern us, to make a better environment for us to live in. Instead they do the opposite and look after themselves. They see it as an opportunity to get richer."

He nods again, in agreement I have to suppose. But he still won't alter his stance.

"You always drive these witch hunts, why won't you now?"

"Like I said it won't change anything. In any case our readers don't want to read these types of stories. They don't care if politicians actually do their jobs and do things for the good of the country. They want stories of gossip, of seeing politicians on a pedestal above them being dragged shamed and embarrassed down to the gutter below."

That's not what I want. I don't want to take pleasure seeing people fail time and again, without trying to change anything. That's his job. I'm doing this for the right reasons. And not just for myself, but to bring change to everybody.

"No, you're wrong."

His hand stops rustling among the papers. I seem to have caught his attention.

"No one cares about those scandals you expose. No one cares whether a politician's had an affair, or is secretly gay. They're not elected to be clean-living in their personal lives. They're elected to do a job. And when they don't do it, there's a problem. When they tell us to be models of society, to be honest, to work hard to earn a living, to abide by the law, but don't do so themselves, then there's a problem. And that's what you have to report."

We stare at each other across the desk. He could stop this if he wanted to. But he doesn't want to, so he won't. I think he personally understands my point but is tied to the knife that butters his bread. To print such stories would constitute a huge shift in the manifesto of the newspaper. Gone would be the front pages reserved for nonsense, scandal and rumour, judged by giant black and white headlines. Gone would be the hyperbole designed to catch the eye and force its way into the consciousness. The paper exists to say something, to let its opinions be known – to not let reporting the news get in the way of commenting on it too. Comments that are then labelled 'the views of the nation.'

No one makes as much money as this man by selling something for 30p, no matter how much the quality of the product or the quantity it sells. This man relies on the money from advertising and also the leeches outside his office waiting to partake in more mutual back scratching, both of which would diminish if my news got the go-ahead. If it wasn't for that, what would the paper actually contain? As long as there's crap flying around, they can still write about it and make money from it.

The buzzing of his intercom interrupts our staring. The secretary outside informs him that some singer's fallen off the wagon. I wonder if what I've told him has made any impact on him at all or whether he'll blindly continue as he's done before. The brightening of his face and gleam in his eyes at the details the secretary routinely reels off, answer my query.

"But printing such stories will change things, I suppose?"

"Look, I realise these kind of stories aren't to your liking, but they are to some. Otherwise why would so many people buy our paper?"

I think back to my Nan and her bundles of chips wrapped in stories about someone having a go at the photographers outside her house when she came home drunk from a party.

"Besides, us showing a celeb drunk or on something shows awareness of the dangers."

"Not when it's you giving it to the celeb when they're trying to give it up."

His eyes fix on me, his back straightens and his throat seems to gulp.

"It's time for you to go now. There's nothing for you here."

And with that I wholeheartedly agree and get up from my seat and walk out the door. As the lift takes me down the 20 floors to the front door of the building, I see myself all alone. If anything's going to be done, it's going to have to begin with me. My mind debates whether I should abrupt my plans altogether.

Chapter Forty Five

It began with me trying to locate the politician. I did this by frequenting various upmarket bars, befriending people I normally wouldn't and listening in on people's conversations. Eventually I found him, which then led to me having a drink or two and a chat with him whenever our paths crossed, which was often seeing as I was going to the bar every night in the hope of meeting him there. None of this was cheap of course, not for me anyway, hence me reading the papers in bed as I've sold the rest of my furniture to pay for these nights out and some smart clothes to go out in.

Not that I always paid for the food, drinks and taxis. "Don't worry, I'll get these." the politician would often say and hand me a fistful of notes, "Just make sure you get a receipt."

The receipts were always neatly placed into the small plastic wallet he kept them in. There were loads in there, thick layers of small pieces of paper, proof of not only such purchases as drinks and taxis but also hotel stays abroad, private flights, petrol. And what he called his 'extra pleasures'. These included the renovation work on his house, the antique furniture he bought, the car he bought as a gift for his darling wife.

There were some things he paid for out of his own pocket, the string of call girls for example, "It's a bit awkward to ask those tarts for a receipt." he told me. And the court injunctions to stop them from telling their stories. "You know, the judge has to decide whether to grant the injunction or not but when he sees who's seeking it and the amount of money I'm paying, then he's left in no doubt." he smugly told me, blowing smoke rings from his cigar.

He showed little remorse for his actions. For him he was losing money. His private businesses were doing badly in the recession and his salary wasn't enough to maintain his lifestyle. "If I have to take a little from elsewhere, then so be it. Everyone does it."

It was great for my project to hear him say such things. Taped to my chest was a microphone which was connected to a tape recorder in my pocket. Every night when I got home I would listen to that night's recording, evaluating the quality of the sound as well as his bragging arrogance. Sometimes I found myself sitting extremely close to him, far too close for comfort, the microphone almost pointed at his mouth, in order to get clear speech from him. Whenever something was inaudible I would just get him to say it again. He didn't need much persuasion to shoot his mouth off about anything.

After about a week or so I got the concern that he could deny it was his voice on the audible recording. Instead I needed his face on camera, with the nonsense spewing visibly from his mouth.

I bought myself one of those tiny cameras like they use in hospitals. Again it was in no way cheap, but it was necessary in the circumstances. I attached it to poke ever so slightly out of my shirt. It was too tiny to be noticed. Even I had trouble spotting it.

I followed him to the bathroom on one occasion and waited in preparation by the sink for him to come out from the cubicle.

"Hey Doug, what are you doing out here?" he bellowed, always striving to be heard everywhere. "Have you come to see whether MP crap smells better than the rest? Ha ha ha!" his red face guffawed. "Of course it does. All that fine dining we have in the Commons." he sniggered. "Wouldn't be possible without the taxpayer, mind." I wish I could say he said this sincerely but a wink of the eye and a tap of the nose never represent sincerity. Still, for what I was after, it wasn't bad.

I set him up to tell me more. I'd heard it all before but he liked telling it again and again.

"What else wouldn't be possible without the taxpayer?"

"Our cars, our lovely homes. All of it pretty much. All from the taxpayers' pay cheque that they've got from stacking crap onto shelves or mopping up piss, or whatever useless job they have because they didn't listen at school."

"Maybe they didn't have doors opened for them."

"Oh, boo hoo! My dad saw to it that I didn't work for scraps like them. If their dads didn't have the right connections, that's tough luck."

I struggle to hide my smile, but I remind myself he doesn't know why I'm smiling.

"What's it like working for government?" I ask him.

"Easiest job in the world, mate." he looks at my face expecting shock horror. I've heard it all before though. "I tell you what, there's never a day when I find myself putting my head down, rushing to get something done. It just doesn't happen. Most of the time I've got my feet up on the desk relaxing or seeing to my wife's cleaning company. The other time's mostly spent in meetings or having liquid lunches. Which are usually the same thing! Ha ha ha! If anything does ever happen, if any shit does hit the fan, that's what the PR men and spin doctors are for. Christ, I couldn't imagine life without them. The bollocks they have to hide…"

"Aha, but…"

"Then they recycle it and make it smell of roses. Ha ha ha!"

After washing his hands and drying them he headed for the exit. To leave though he would have to pass me, something which I wasn't prepared to let him do.

"Hold on a minute there." I said and placed my hand on his shoulder. "Have a look at this."

I pulled the iphone out of my pocket and put it between us so we both could watch. I however was more interested in watching his reaction. I saw his face get redder, his lips drier and beads of sweat form on the top of his forehead.

"I'll give you anything for that right now. Anything. Whatever you want." his voice suddenly drained of its cocksureness and filled with panic.

It amused me that he should be so scared of people seeing him say such things when they already suspect and expect it. I smiled and wondered just how far he would go to get it. It wasn't my aim to gain any money or expensive gifts, nor was it to see him squirm. But why shouldn't I take advantage of his fear? There was still more I wanted from this.

"I want you to apologise and beg forgiveness."

A look of surprise seemed to brighten his ashen face. Surprise maybe at the small punishment he would have to face.

"Of course, I'm sorry. I'm so sorry. Please forgive me."

"No, no. Stand over there and say it to the camera."

He looked at me unsure of whether I was serious or not. But I was deadly serious. And he was going to know it. I gave him a piece of paper with something I'd prepared earlier. This was to be his script.

"Stand over there and tell the camera how you abuse the privileges that have been bestowed on you by people that you loathe and ridicule; that the peoples' problems don't matter as long as you're doing ok; that millions are harmed by your decisions, soldiers die because you wanted a war, people live in poverty because you screwed the economy. Then beg for forgiveness."

He looked at the ground and slowly nodded his head. His fate had been accepted it seemed.

"And a lot of people are going to see this, so be sincere and honest."

He hesitantly and slowly made his way over to the wall opposite. He stood himself straight and took a deep breath. I focused the camera and gave him the go-ahead to begin.

"Hello. My name is Robert Dawson MP."

It was a good start and so it continued. He reeled off everything that was on the piece of paper as well as all he'd told me during our rendezvous in brutal, deadpan honesty. Plus there was something new about how lucky he was to work in government. But not because of the honour of responsibility, but because it meant he could earn so much for doing so little. And he didn't only mean the salary and expenses, but also the power, the influence and the status.

"We often have to put on a determined face and promise a rightful intention, but then that's followed by an explanation – usually fictitious – of our failure to deliver. It's often the case that we couldn't care less about fulfilling our promises. While there are still problems in this country, there will be promises made to rectify them. And the parties will argue with each other to convince you of the best solution. If we did everything that we said we would then there wouldn't be any problems and you wouldn't have any need for us at all."

It was then he looked away from the camera and gave me a glance. I agreed that that was enough and switched the camera off. He came back over towards me and compassionately touched my left arm.

"Please Doug, I'm begging you now. Don't go anywhere with that. Let me keep hold of it."

There was a definite feel of desperation in his eyes and his voice.

"What will happen if I take this to the newspapers?" Of course I already knew the answer and had no intention of going to any newspaper.

"It will ruin me. I'll be sacked and will never get a job in politics again. Probably won't get a job anywhere. Not a top one anyway."

"And you'll lose your privileges and lifestyle."

He nodded furiously like a child begging to keep his favourite toy.

My original plan was to take the video to the newspapers. I don't normally approve of those newspaper 'stings', especially when it's some singer or actor being recorded admitting to an error they've committed or a secret they've held. In most cases I don't believe it's in the public's interest to know, or care for that matter. More often than not they're an awful betrayal of trust and faith and just a ploy to create news and sell more papers.

But this was a story worth telling. And they weren't interested. I needed a different tactic.

"What if I do give it you, what will happen then?"

His face perked up ever so slightly, like a child who's just got a glimmer that everything's going to be alright.

"How do we know we won't be back here in this situation again?"

"I'll change, I'll change, I promise!"

"You'll change?"

"Everything! I'll take the job seriously and give it the respect it deserves."

I believed him. Something in his face told me he meant it.

"I'll tell you what. I won't go to the press with the video. Nor will I post it online."

He sighed with huge relief, his body visibly relaxing in front of me.

"But I won't give it to you. It will remain secure with me."

His eyes flash back to me. I think his mind had briefly wandered elsewhere when I told him I wouldn't sell the video.

"In return, you must give your job the utmost dedication it deserves. Eliminate corruption and idleness, create jobs for the unemployed, build homes for the homeless, give people a reason to live and be proud. Give them an alternative to drugs, crime and worthlessness."

He nods his head, seemingly stirred by what I've said.

"And if I find you slacking, then 1 or 50 million people will hear about our little chat here tonight.

Agreed?"

Chapter Forty Six

I lie now in bed, thinking my final thoughts of the day. It won't be long until I'm sound asleep. It's been a busy few weeks trying to realise my place in the world, to justify my life, but in the end it's given me a great feeling of satisfaction. I feel satisfied with doing something to help someone else, to help many people. Maybe nothing will come of it, I'll have to keep tabs on them, but at least I've done something. And that's a lot more than those who moan about things have done – a group to which I used to belong. Why did I moan about such unimportant things? Where did it ever get me?

Such bliss isn't cheap though and it's all come at a cost. My pockets have been spared the weight of carrying cash and my bank balance is just about displaying 3 figures. My wish to have my own café or hostel is as long a way off as ever. The moonlight shines through my window at my empty room, now rid of furniture and any valuable possessions. But then how valuable and necessary is money when your conscience is clear and your soul is healthy?

My eyes are flickering now. I suppose the time to sleep has arrived.

Chapter Forty Seven

Almost as soon as my eyes flicker shut they flicker open again, I'm waking up now. I've had a nice sleep with no interruptions except some beeping I thought I could hear earlier. But that's stopped now and my eyes are open to see a bright light shine through the window behind me. The sky is as blue as it can be and everything is illuminated by it, including the room where I lay. I look at the ceiling; it's an extra shade of white today. A brighter shade. It doesn't get much whiter than this. I lay still for a minute, enjoying and appreciating the moment. The sun is shining, the sky is clear, birds are singing outside, it's a fine day. Everything feels within my grasp. The world is my oyster.

For a tiny second I feel something brush against my cheek. As quickly as I feel it, it's gone. Maybe it was… No, I don't know what it could've been. But there it is again petting the side of my face and now stroking my hair. I turn to the side and see Michaela sitting beside my bed.
She's crying, quite a lot actually. She's not even trying to hide it or stem the flow. I look at one of her wet bloodshot eyes and see a tear drop from it. The tear runs from the eye, down beside her nose, rising to the tip of her cheek before falling off her face and onto the floor. I look over to the other eye and see the same thing happen.

Standing in the corner behind Michaela my parents are talking to someone. I can't make out who it is. They're a bit too far away from my bed for me to see clearly. I didn't realise my room was so big. My mum's ducked her head and I can get a better view now. I think that's Adam, the doctor from the hospital. What's he doing here?

Whatever he's said to my mum and dad, they're not happy. My mum's crying and my dad's holding her and turning his back on Dr Adam.

I look up at the ceiling again, it really is bright today, almost magical. I should make sure I remember it because this is the last time I'll see this room.

"It's time." a voice from somewhere says. Before I can look around to place it, the bed sheet is pulled over my head.

For the next few minutes I can feel my bed move, pushed down a corridor. I can't see anything and can only hear muffled sounds. I hear what sounds like lift doors closing and then a robot voice announcing that the doors are opening to the basement.

I can vaguely hear a person's voice. A man's. It's probably the person pushing me around. He says he'll be home soon and something about stopping off at KFC. He just needs to drop one more stiff off in the morgue.

Then there's the robot voice again, this time announcing that the doors are closing. I suddenly feel something crash into either side of the bed, making it shake for a few seconds. The man makes a noise, it sounds like a tut, before moving me again, pulling the sheet off my right foot as he does so. I feel a draught engulf me, it's cold down here.

The man says he doesn't know what happened, he only pushes things around and doesn't ask questions. But he thinks this one had a funny turn during the night. He starts to laugh and say that he can't leave him in the lift because he'd get the sack. Even if the stiff's got nothing planned and is in no hurry.

Lightning Source UK Ltd.
Milton Keynes UK
UKOW031807110113

204775UK00001B/3/P